We thoroughly enjoyed reading *Stranger in the Pulpit*. The story, which includes suspense, gunfights, and a clever antagonist, kept us reading to that last page. We know you will like the characters and plot of this exciting story.

—Reagan and Madison Pritt
(Teen and Tween, respectively)

Stranger in the Pulpit deals with doctrinal issues from a conservative point-of-view. It is a great book to give someone who is struggling with some of the New Age and emerging church practices that are creeping into the church. While treating all these issues, it delivers an exciting plot, interesting characters, and a lot of action!

—Rev. Jimmy and Eileen Stallard,
Treasures of Truth Ministries.
Authors of *Facing the Sons of Thunder,*
Praying Through Adversity,
and *Faith For Your Fears*

STRANGER

IN THE

PULPIT

THE
STRANGER SERIES

STRANGER
IN THE
PULPIT

To Carol
Happy reading

BRYAN M. POWELL

TATE PUBLISHING & *Enterprises*

Published by Tate Publishing & Enterprises, LLC
127 E. Trade Center Terrace | Mustang, Oklahoma 73064 USA
1.888.361.9473 | www.tatepublishing.com

Tate Publishing is committed to excellence in the publishing industry. The company reflects the philosophy established by the founders, based on Psalm 68:11,
"The Lord gave the word and great was the company of those who published it."

Published in the United States of America

ISBN: 978-1-61346-042-9
Fiction: Religious
11.07.12

DEDICATION

I give God the glory and thanks for giving me a message and a way of expressing it.

I dedicate this book to pastor Dr. T.P. Johnston for his extensive study on the Emergent Church and the New Age Movement. His teaching provided me with a wealth of information needed that formed the basis for this book.

I give much thanks to my wife, Patty, for enduring my absence as I spent long hours writing this and the succeeding books of this trilogy, and doing the first two editorial readings.

Thanks to Eileen Stallard for being my first editor in chief. I told her to be merciless in her editing and she was.

Thanks to Courtney Martin and Tina Roberts for being my last line of defense as they did a heroic job in the final edit process.

CHARACTER BIOGRAPHIES

Chase Newton–a 25 year old investigative reporter with the *Beaumont Observer*. Good looking, athletic, a traditionalist.

Megan Richards–the beautiful daughter of Pastor T.J. Richards.

Stan Berkowitz–Editor and Chief of the *Beaumont Observer, Beaumont, Colorado*

Glenn Tibbits–a modern day Mordecai, retired 60-year-old jeweler and a pillar in the community.

Sheriff Conyers–long time resident of Beaumont, Colorado. He was not a happy camper. He was upset with the disregard of common decency for the law of the land...his land...his laws.

John Wiener–a recent newcomer to Beaumont. A land developer, closing attorney, and member of The Order.

Ann Conley–the new president of the First National Bank of Beaumont. A Deaconess and hard-core member of The Order.

Pastor T.J. Richards–the new pastor of Community First Church and Head of the Table of The Order. His wife is Estella the daughter of the Ambassador to Yemen.

Susan Bailes–bank examiner.

Jimmy Stevens–one of the bank employees, envious and revengeful, who stumbles across something of great value to The Order.

Luke Cooley–a high school drop-out, and the son of Deputy Cooley. He has a way of solving other people's problems.

The Order–a clandestine, quasi-religious movement with ties to the Middle East. They had big plans for the United States of America.

The Document–The Title Deed to a large tract of land the size of the Mid-West. Someone got sloppy or greedy or both.

Introduction to Stranger in the Pulpit

"For such [are] false apostles, deceitful workers, transforming themselves into the apostles of Christ. And no marvel; for Satan himself is transformed into an angel of light. Therefore [it is] no great thing if his ministers also be transformed as the ministers of righteousness; whose end shall be according to their works."

II Corinthians 11:13–15

CHAPTER 1

The Beaumont Observer

Only an ostrich with her head in the sand could miss the fact that change was coming. In the world outside of our sleepy town of Beaumont, change had already come. Ever since the November election, the political landscape has changed, and the culture all around us is feeling it; even the civility of common people was changing.

> Change comes slowly to Beaumont, but it was coming!

This was how the editorial for the *Beaumont Observer* began as Chase Newton, the hotshot cub reporter, wrote it.

Beaumont was a sleepy ski resort town of forty-five thousand tucked away in the mountains of Colorado. Its only claim to fame is its association with two bank robbers who robbed The First National Bank of Beaumont over one hundred years ago. In honor of that infamous day, the city fathers named the streets intersecting the city square after them. One street was named Butch Cassidy Drive and the other Sundance Strip. The other two streets carried the names of the gang they led and the place that they called home. They were Wild Bunch Way and Robber's Roost Street. The four streets were tree-lined, and there was a large fountain in the middle of the square. This is where the town gathered for its annual Fourth of July picnic and barbecue. The name Beaumont or "beautiful hill" evokes the idea of nostalgia, of tradition, of a way of life. That was then!

The *Observer* as it was commonly called, was an old-line rag dating back to the early 1930s. Although the building that housed the paper was old and crumbling, there had been a lot of new improvements made to the infrastructure. There were new computers, printers, and a state-of-the-art multicolor Davison Diddle Printing Press. With the exception of the squeaky floors and the strong smell of ink, the *Observer* appeared to be catching up to the twentieth century, except it was 2003!

Chase, dressed in a golf shirt, khaki slacks, and casual shoes, was fairly new to the *Observer*, but he certainly was not new to the reporting business. Actually, Chase was quite a veteran. When it comes to scooping out a hot story, Chase was one of the best. At age twenty-five, he had already developed quite a reputation. His only competition was the talk show hosts who seemed to have the ability of exhausting a topic long before he had a chance to weigh in on it. So, Chase had to be content and wait. Wait and try to catch the next story before it became a story. That was his stock and trade, looking for trends and latching on to them, nurturing them along. It wasn't that Chase was in favor of all the trends he saw. He just needed them as badly as they needed him. Actually, Chase was a traditionalist. Brought up in North Carolina, he felt the strong influences of his godly, Bible-believing parents. And though he didn't subscribe to their belief system, he at least had a foundation—a worldview that was traditional. That put him at odds with his former journalism school at the University of North Carolina. It also put him in an unusual and sometimes tenuous position with his senior editor, Stan Berkowitz.

If you were to cross the character that Ed Asner played on the Mary Tyler Moore Show with the personalities of a porcupine and skunk, you might come close to Stan Berkowitz. That his personality was renowned goes without saying, but so was his ability to drive his reporters to new heights, or new lows, depending on your perspective. The one thing Stan had going for him was his love of a good story. If he thought you were on to something big, all the resources of the *Observer* were behind you. And today, Chase was basking in those benefits.

"Chase, have you noticed the number of new residents in town lately? This isn't even the peak season and already we are having traffic jams," Stan said as he and Chase worked on a box of donuts.

The street outside of the *Observer* was tree-lined; the old sidewalk, rippled as the roots of the trees pushed it up. It had been home to the newspaper for as long as most people could remember.

"Yes!" said Chase, "I was crossing the street down from the post office and nearly got run over by a black SUV with Virginia tags. There's not only a lot more people than usual, but they're rude too. Some blond just waved her hand as if I was in the wrong for crossing in front of her. She had a lot of nerve."

"What's the occasion? It's not anywhere near the ski season. And I know the new Wal-Mart on the outskirts of town isn't bringing in that many folks," Stan said, leaning back in his chair.

"I don't know. Even the old downtown church seems to be benefiting as well."

"That old building? That church has been in decline for years. I figured they would have closed their doors by now."

The First Church, as it was called, was made up of a series of buildings taking up a whole city block right on the corner of the town square. Its belfry rang out the hour of the day, every day. It was part of the atmosphere of the town. In a way, people grew to expect the old bell to ring, and if for some mysterious reason it didn't ring, people seemed a little off schedule. The church, at least its bell, gave stability to the city.

"I drove by there last Saturday night," Chase said, "and the parking lot was filled, and people were using the Dollar General's parking lot as overflow. It sounded like a rock concert going on in there. I could hear it from the street."

"Chase, I think you need to look into why all these people are coming to Beaumont. You need to do a 'Man on the Street' interview. Our readership could use a shot in the arm, and some local news might pique their interest."

The *Observer* itself was feeling the effects of the economic downturn, too. Readership was declining, costs were rising, and the paper was feeling the pinch.

"Well, at least the 'talk-show guys' aren't talking about this," Chase said ruefully. "Maybe I can puff the story, and it'll get picked up by the *Colorado Review*. I've already started working on my next editorial using that as the basis. Listen to this title: 'What's New In Town?'"

Stan crossed his arms in front of his robust chest and frowned. "Go for it, kid, but you gotta work on the leading title."

Chase was not the only person who had observed the subtleties of change. Like the earliest nuances of fall, so were the changes within the Community First Church as Glenn Tibbits noticed. Glenn had had his fill of change. Most of it was only cosmetic—the rearranging of the furniture, and he went along with it. Even the church's name change was acceptable to Glenn. The old downtown First Church had been in decline long before its former pastor resigned. Now, under new leadership came a new name, a facelift, and many new faces. That wasn't all that bad according to the few remaining old-timers. As long as the coffers were full and the pews were full, everything was fine in Beaumont.

Those observable changes were not what concerned Glenn. Glenn had been brought up in the First Church. He had been saved, baptized, and eventually ordained as a deacon. He returned after being gone about ten years, but for most of his sixty years, he spent them there, teaching, singing, and otherwise maintaining the church. To most people, he was the pillar, which held the old church up.

That was then!

Now the church, under new management, was subject to new ideas: some not particularly bad, just different. A change of name, a different order of services, even the livelier music didn't bother Glenn. As a matter of fact, Glenn was the one responsible for bringing in the new pastor.

CHAPTER 2

The Community First Church

Pastor T.J. Richards, or T.J. as he preferred being called, was a well-groomed, forty-five-year-old veteran of the ministry. Ever since he graduated from Bruton College, Summa Cum Laude, twenty-five years ago, he had built an impeccable résumé. His former haunts included all of the step-up and move-up churches one would need if he wanted to be at the top of the religious ladder. Glenn only knew his name through a mutual friend back east. His résumé, however, looked solid. Plus, he won the majority of the search committee's hearts with his closed-door sermon, packed with homespun illustrations, facts and anecdotal information.

The vote was scheduled for the last Sunday night in August; Glenn called the meeting to order and acted as moderator. After the reading of the minutes from the last business meeting by the secretary, the budget was read by the treasurer. Glenn spoke up and said, "I move to elect Reverend T.J. Richards as our new pastor. Do we have a second?" John Wiener seconded the motion.

"Do we have any questions or discussion?" the moderator said.

One elderly woman raised her hand and was quickly recognized by Glenn. "I recognize Ms. Emma."

Ms. Emma Baxter was probably the godliest woman in the county, maybe the whole state of Colorado. It was said of Ms. Emma that she spent over half the day praying for her church, her family and friends, and for her country. She asked just one question and took her seat. "Have we prayed and fasted over this decision?"

No one spoke; they could have heard a pin drop on carpet. The reason why no one spoke was obvious—they didn't pray nor had they fasted. To most of the voting members, T.J. and his family looked and sounded like the perfect family to lead their church. Who needed to pray about the obvious? The vote was a virtual landslide. Over 95 percent of the voting membership ruled in favor of Pastor T.J., with one objection: Ms. Emma.

After the votes were counted, Glenn announced the results. "Well, church family, it looks like we have us a pastor."

Pastor T.J. was in the lobby, waiting for the vote to be taken. Glenn stuck his head into the lobby and smiled, "Brother T.J., it looks like you have a church, if you'll have us."

T.J. just smiled back and said, "Wonderful, let's get to work."

Within a few weeks the new pastor moved his family into some temporary housing. The new parsonage would not be completed for another three months. Until then, they would have to make do. At the same time, Pastor T.J. set into motion a series of steps, which he hoped would move the church forward. It was an exciting time in the life of the church as new faces and new money began to come into the church. By the time the first family was moved into the mansion they called the parsonage, the pastor was ready to implement an aggressive program for growth.

"Now that we are moved into the new parsonage, I've sent plans to my architect on improvements to the church facility," T.J. said to Glenn as they went out for lunch at Maxine's Diner.

"This is the first I've heard about any renovations. Don't we need to vote on it?"

"Glenn, my friend, voting on every little change I plan on making will only slow down the process and impede our future growth. You don't want to be perceived as someone standing in the way of growth now, do ya?"

Glenn certainly didn't want to get on the bad side of the pastor so soon, and so he went along to get along.

Over the next months, many of the renovation projects were completed including a facelift on the street side, an enlarged platform area, new seats replacing the old pews, and an upgraded sound system. At the same time, the church had broken ground for the new administration wing, which replaced the old Sunday school building. This would include a new pastor's study, conference room and other administrative offices.

"Pastor, I had no idea that a simple name change would attract so many people, and so young!" Glenn said as he and the new pastor sat in the original pastor's study.

"Glenn, my friend," said the pastor warmly, "at your age, everyone looks young."

"Yes, but so many of them are buying homes and settling in. Where are they finding work? The ski season is months away and most of those jobs are minimum wage. How can these people afford to be buying new homes?

"Well, you know what the good book says, 'God helps those who help themselves.'"

Glenn scratched the back on his neck and said, "I don't recall reading that verse in my King James Version."

"Oh, it's there all right, it's in the new RDV, the Reader's Digest Version."

Glenn quietly nodded and walked away.

Pastor T.J.'s aura was not the only factor in the overwhelming vote. So was his stylish wife, Estella. What church would not want her as their First Lady? Her charismatic personality and speaking ability would have carried the day even if Brother T.J. flopped. What a combination!

And then there was Megan.

If any two people could come together and produce an angel it was T.J. and Estella. Megan, now twenty-one, was their only child. While her father studied the eastern religions in some of the prominent universities in the Middle East, Megan was being educated in Muslim schools. When her family moved back to the U.S. she finished her education at the noted Norrington Finishing School located in Arlington Heights, Virginia. As a right of passage, her twenty-first birthday celebration was to be noteworthy, even for the *Observer*.

Not only were all of the church members invited, but all of the city fathers all the way down to the dogcatcher. While Megan's birthday bash was not on Chase's beat, the mere size of the event didn't pass his notice. Since she was the editor of her local junior college newspaper, Megan had consulted Chase on several occasions on word-sculpturing over the past year. That and the occasional clandestine rendezvous over an ice cream sundae kept Chase interested in what was happening in Megan's life. What wasn't news to most folks in a town of 45,000 became news, especially if it included a reporter.

CHAPTER 3

The Richard's Home

"Great party, Megan! Happy Birthday!"

Megan, dressed in a light green stylish gown, was stunning to look at; blond, shapely, athletic, and the most available twenty-one-year old in the county. She turned around and smiled back at Chase, and said, "Hey stranger, I'm glad you could make it. I've never seen so many people in one place."

She is gorgeous, Chase thought.

"Yeah, and a lot of the big shots in town have crashed the party, too."

"Oh, no, Daddy invited them, he invited everybody," she said gleefully.

"That's great, M, but how can he afford a bash this size on a preacher's budget?"

"Oh, he just stepped out on faith and trusted God to do the rest. He has this motto, something about 'God helps those who'…uh well you know," her voice trailing off.

"I see!" though he didn't. "Do you want something to eat?" Chase offered.

"Yes, just as long as I don't drop something on this gown. How do you like it?"

Chase stepped back to get a better look. "It's stupendous, M, you look marvelous."

"Oh, Chase, are all reporters as good with words as you are?" Megan said as she blushed.

"I had to go to school to learn multi-syllable words such as stupendous and multiculturalism."

"Multiculturalism, is that the same thing as mixing rich people and poor people?" Megan asked lightly.

"Yeah, maybe, sort of like tonight, you got a dukes mixture of everybody here," Chase said as he scanned the crowd.

"Speaking of that, we've been having a lot of people come to our Saturday night 'P and W' services. Why not join us this weekend?"

Chase looking rather confused asked, "What's a 'P and W' service?"

"You know, a praise and worship service. It's our version of church, only it's on Saturday evening. It's designed to attract young people."

"I'll think about it, but no promises. I don't want to commit and let you down. Plus, I have a deadline I gotta meet at midnight on Saturday." He lied; the deadline was at noon on Saturday.

Although Chase was basically a traditionalist, he wasn't an actual believer. And despite Megan's continued invitations to come to their praise and worship services, Chase found it difficult to commit to faithful or even semi-regular attendance. His occasional visits only brought confusion. What seemed clear to him, as a boy growing up in a deeply religious home, now became questions without answers, problems without solutions, and quests without quarries. So, Chase's journey began. At first it didn't seem like a journey. He could take it or leave it, or could he? Something was drawing him and it wasn't just Megan.

Now, after visiting a few Saturday nights in a row, Chase realized that there was something different about Pastor T.J. Was it just his imagination? Was it just his childhood recollection playing tricks on him? *What was so different about Pastor T.J.?* Chase asked himself as he drove home in his old, beat-up Jeep Cherokee. What was it that he was teaching that brought him to question what little he knew of the Bible?

What made it even more confusing was the way Megan so fully supported her parent's teaching, or so he thought. Not like himself, who just couldn't or wouldn't get it when his dad shouted "Amen" to the rhythm of the guest preacher. Neither did he understand his mom at times. She would sing every verse of every song, same tempo, same volume, loud and fast! Chase, nicknamed after his uncle, could still remember those nights when the early evening prayer meeting turned into an all-nighter. And so, as an eighteen-year-old, he struck out on his own; first working as a messenger boy in the mailroom at the *Raleigh Post,* then enrolling in the University of North Carolina with a major in journalism. Four years later his only regret was that his dad didn't live to see him graduate. The effects of Alzheimer's had taken his mom. She was just a shell of the person she once was, a well-read, well-spoken woman. She left a legacy behind of a woman of courage and character. Many were the times that Chase wished he could go back and talk with his dad and mom.

That was not possible now.

If there were answers to be found, Chase would have to find them himself. In a way, he envied Megan. She seemed to have all the answers, at least the answers to the prescribed questions. If she ever got off script, she was as lost as he was.

CHAPTER 4

The Community First Church

At first Glenn passed it off as a different approach, a different interpretation. But the longer he listened, the more he wondered. And the more he wondered, the more he questioned. Those questions remained within the mainframe of his mind. He had observed what happened to those who voiced their questions. Charges of insubordination and lack of loyalty were brought to bear. Those who continued their quest for answers were summarily dismissed from the membership. Those smart enough, or weak enough, quickly learned to keep their heads down and their mouths shut.

Chase parked his Jeep in a parking slot marked "Visitor Parking" and got out. He made his way into the lobby of the old church, dressed casually, as Megan told him, "Nobody wears ties to church anymore, and if you want to wear blue jeans, that's fine by me. The tighter the better."

This was the atmosphere that Chase faced as he drove to the Saturday evening praise and worship service. He entered the foyer of the newly remodeled sanctuary rather reluctantly. The aroma of freshly brewed coffee filled the room, giving a warm, homey feeling. In a way he dreaded what was coming. If it were anything like what he was used to, he'd leave as soon as they started passing the hat. He met Megan in the lobby by the coffee shop called Perks.

Perks was one of those improvements thought to attract young people. If the demographers knew anything, they knew their young people. The lobby of the old church was a-buzz with young teens and college-aged people. They even had WI-FI, and several were logged on and were surfing the Internet. Others stood there texting their friends who were just yards away.

"Hey M, how's it going?" Chase noticed she had taken her own advice.

Megan looked up, her smile lit up the dimly lit coffee shop.

"Hey stranger, thought you weren't coming. Did ya make your deadline?"

"Yeah. I made it with plenty of time and ole Berkowitz will be happy till Monday when the race starts all over again."

"I don't know how you do it, coming up with a story every week, week in and week out."

"Believe me, it ain't easy. Want some coffee?"

"Yeah, let's."

"What did you write about this week?" Megan asked as she stirred her latté.

"It's entitled, 'The Economic Downturn, Turns Around.' It's about how the economy around here is turning around for the good. By the looks of it, there is lots of money available for the good life in this town. Maybe the article will attract even more people to move here. With crime at an all-time low and new businesses popping up all around, it seems like a good time to run the article. I think even the Chamber of Commerce will use parts of it in their new brochure."

They spent the next forty-five minutes in Perks chatting about what Megan wanted to do with her life now that she was a big twenty-one-year-old woman. Then they slipped into some seats near the back of the sanctuary close to the door and the restroom. He had consumed copious amounts of coffee waiting for the band to finally run out of steam. They took their seats near an elderly man to Chase's right. The older gentlemen reminded Chase of someone he once knew. There was a confidence about him. His presence exuded humility, wisdom, and patience. There was an immediate kindred spirit knit between the two and not a word was spoken. Not so with Megan; there was just something Megan didn't like about Glenn. She knew she didn't like him, but just couldn't put her finger on it.

"Come on, Chase, let's see if we can find another area to sit in."

"Why, M? What's wrong with these seats?"

Looking across Chase at the elderly man, Megan said, "Let's just say I'd like to sit where the air is much fresher."

Chase looked over at the elderly gentleman and shrugged his shoulders apologetically as Megan pulled Chase's arm and led him to the opposite side of the sanctuary.

The old sanctuary had been completely renovated. There were special lights hanging from the ceiling, lights for the enlarged stage as well. The new state-of-the-art Bose speaker system, complete with surround sound, made it feel that the music was coming from all sides; and it was! The old pews had been removed and new interlocking padded chairs replaced them.

"You can get a lot more people in this place by using chairs rather than those uncomfortable pews," Megan said as they found their new seats.

The place was packed. They barely found two seats together. The overhead screen descended from a slot in the ceiling and lit up with the lyrics of a familiar praise and worship chorus, which all but Chase seemed to know. After standing and singing the same song over and over again the praise team disbanded, leaving the stage.

Pastor T.J. strode out from behind the curtain to the sound of applause. Dressed in a casual open-collared shirt, shorts, and sandals, T.J. looked more ready to go to a ball game than a church service. The sermon began with his usual greeting: "Good evening, I come to you bringing greetings from all that is good and decent in the world."

Was that a slight British accent or was it just my imagination? Chase thought to himself.

"Today we will continue the conversation we've been having by asking one of Jesus' famous questions. You know, Jesus never really preached a sermon as you and I think of it. Preaching as we grew up hearing doesn't work! It just turns people off! So, let's have a civil conversation. Let's ask questions and let's see if we can't come up with some better results."

The reverb on his over-the-ear microphone, which was barely visible, gave his voice an almost god-like sound.

Chase's ears perked up. He liked this guy.

"And so let's discuss this question that Jesus asked, 'Who do people say that I am?'"

Pastor T.J. had left the platform area and mingled among the crowd.

"You know if *he* didn't know who he was, how did he expect anyone else to know who he was?"

He paused to let the laughter subside. His timing was impeccable. He should have been a stand-up comedian. He could have gone all night like this.

"Seriously, let's get back to the topic we're discussing and see if we can't come up with some answers. Let me see a show of hands. Who was Jesus? Hmm, okay, yes, I heard someone yell 'Elijah.' Let's have another…okay, you there, in the red t-shirt…he said, 'John the Baptist.' You see, Jesus never denied any of these answers. He didn't condemn anyone for giving those answers. As a matter of fact, he said, '…neither do I condemn you,' John 8:11 (ESV). So, what can we come away from this with? Yes, I see that hand, hmm, uh huh, yes. 'That Jesus can be who-ever you say he is,'" he repeated. "That's right! You can call him Jesus, Allah, Mohammad, Buddha, whatever best represents your concept of God. You see, even in the Old Testament God went by many names. Jehovah, Elohim,

Yahweh, El Shaddai, I Am. You know, the Old Testament God of the Bible had followers from many cultures. There were the Philistines; there was Naaman from Damascus, even the Queen of Sheba. So, let's not get hung up on viewing Jesus through just the Judeo-Christian sunglasses. Let's see if we can find truth in other places. And when, *not if*, but *when* we find it, *embrace it*! For the search for truth is our highest calling. Let's join with Pontius Pilot of old and ask ourselves: 'What is Truth?'"

The damage was done!

What began as a question grew to a suspicion. Chase had to find out the "Who, What, Where, and Why" of what was happening down at the Community First Church.

Chase leaned over and quietly whispered, "That was quite an eye-opener. Your dad said a lot of pretty deep stuff; it got me thinking."

"Yeah, Dad's a pretty cool guy, even if he *is* my dad."

"Well, he said some stuff I heard my dad say, but this time it seemed to make more sense. But I still have a lot of questions."

"I guess that's why you're the investigative reporter."

"Yeah, I'm hopelessly doomed to a life of questions. Look, it's getting late. I gotta go." Chase turned to go.

"Will I see you next week?"

"Now look who's got the questions," Chase said with a smile.

He avoided the answer.

CHAPTER 5

The Beaumont Observer

Monday morning, Chase sat staring at his computer screen. He still didn't get it. He had written the opening lines of his next article, but hit a brick wall. There were just too many questions, too many loose ends. He needed more answers.

He needed more time!

The only way to get to the bottom of this dilemma and maybe, just maybe, get to the top of my profession is to go undercover, he thought. *I need to become one of them, to get on the inside, to get behind the veil. In order for me to do that, I am going to need the backing of my editor, Stan, and a recommendation for membership.* It seemed that with the notoriety of the Community First Church came a more guarded approach to membership.

Chase needed a good story to explain why he suddenly changed his position from being a cool agnostic to a rabid believer. He had to sell Megan and he needed an ally on the inside to have credibility when he broke the story.

He didn't know it yet, but he needed Glenn.

"That story last week was a blast to write," Chase said as he grabbed a fresh donut from the box that Stan brought in. "But it didn't really answer all of my questions."

Stan set the box down on Chase's cluttered desk, and leaned against the wall. "Want some coffee to go with that?" Stan said as he began looking for his favorite jelly donut. "Questions such as?"

"Such as, who is hiring these people? To look at them, they seem to be above middle class; they drive two cars, their kids dress well, and the golf courses on Sundays always have foursomes backed up.

"So that's your beef, you can't get a decent tee-time?"

Chase was a golfer ever since his dad introduced him to the game back in his teenage years. When he left home and started working, Sunday turned into fun day for Chase as he changed his priorities. Since then Sunday was *his* day, and he filled it with *his* agenda: sleeping in and playing golf.

"No, not really, I just got a funny feeling about this. Where's the new industry? They couldn't all be 'work-from homers' or 'stay-at-home dads.' I checked, and a lot of the license plates are coming from back east," Chase noted.

"Maybe they are fleeing the cities, fearing what happened to Chicago and Detroit will happen to them. You know, I heard that foreign interests were buying up land tracts like they were hotcakes."

Chase thought for a moment. "I've heard that too for years, but that can't be. Who would want old, rusty, uninhabited cities? There's nothing of value there, all but the poorest of the poor live there. The depression went deeper then anyone ever expected."

"And longer. It cost the president his reelection," Stan noted.

"Yeah, and this new guy is willing to give away the kitchen and the kitchen sink to keep the wolves away from our front door."

Stan leaned forward and looked over his glasses, "So getting back to your 'feeling'; in my short time of knowing you I've noticed that you have a nose for a good story."

"I do, so let me throw this at you. Why don't I go undercover? You know, join the ranks of the 'believers' and see where it leads me?"

Stan crossed his arms and stroked his stubbly chin. "You might be fairly new in town, but people already know you ain't no saint. I got all sort of flack from some of my long-time readers about that article you wrote a month ago. No way will those people let you anywhere near the front door of a church, let alone *that church*. What's its name, Community First Church?"

Chase ran his hand though his sandy blond hair. "We need a cover story."

"A cover story! This ain't the CIA, son! Newspapers don't make up stories, they report the news."

"What planet did you just get off of? Since when didn't newspapers make up stories?"

Stan, who was getting hot under the collar for being upbraided by an underling, said, "You know what I mean, we don't make up stories about ourselves ... *most of the time*," his voice trailing off.

"So okay, for the sake of argument, what's your idea of a cover story gonna be?" Stan asked crossing his arms as he took a quick look at his wristwatch. "Are you gonna quit over principles or over irreconcilable differences of opinions? Heck, if that were the case, I'd have to quit too; I don't agree with myself half the time."

"Okay, let's pick a topic and agree to disagree. What's hot on the national scene?" Chase turned to his computer and Googled 'news.'

"Well, the Supreme Court just came out with a ruling on the 'Free Speech Issue,' that's hot," Stan said off the top of his head

"Yeah, but everybody knows that newspaper guys are for free speech. Right?" asked Chase as he looked at the computer.

"Do you think people should be allowed to say anything, anywhere, anytime?"

Chase thought about that a moment. "Well, yes ... most of the time."

Stan uncrossed his arms and stuck his hands out, "There, you see, you don't agree; *we don't agree!*"

"You mean to say Stan, that you think people should be allowed to say anything, anytime, anywhere?"

"Yes, I think people should be allowed to say anything, anywhere, anytime *period.* No restrictions!"

"Nope, I disagree, people shouldn't be allowed to say anything, anywhere! For example, in a movie theater, some wise guy shouldn't be allowed to yell 'Fire' if there isn't one!"

"The Constitution doesn't specify that, and you know it."

Stan was getting hot. He was on a roll. It's never a good idea to pick an argument with your boss, even if it was hypothetical.

Stan said with a chuckle, "Well, there you have it, we don't agree, so you're fired! Pack up your stuff and get your tail outta here."

Chase, rather taken aback, wasn't sure if Stan was kidding or serious. He turned and stomped off, slamming the door behind him.

It wasn't long before the headline on the front cover above the fold read: "Rookie Reporter Fired over Principles."

Stan ran multiple follow-up articles and was sure to include the letters to the editor, both pro and con. That put Chase on the outs with the paper and on the *ins* with the law-abiding people of Beaumont. Even Glenn and Pastor T.J., who seldom agreed on much anymore, agreed on this.

CHAPTER 6

The Pastor's Study

"Have you been reading about the reporter from the Observer getting fired?" Glenn said as he and the pastor sat in the pastor's newly remodeled office. *An office! They call this an office!* Glenn thought to himself. This was no office that Glenn had ever seen. The room was huge. The walls were lined with bookshelves. In between the bookshelves were paintings by the famous western artist Charles Russell. There were sculptures and large vases filled with real flower arrangements. A twenty-foot glass-topped conference table filled one half of the room. There also was a lounge area. The desk where Pastor T.J. sat would have made any CEO proud to sit behind, but this was in a preacher's office? Glenn sat in wonderment.

"Yes! Yes, I have. The young man stood up on principles and that goes a long way in my book," he sat back and piously folded his hands as if praying.

"Yeah, well it got him fired and probably put out on the street. With all these new folks getting all the jobs, I suspect that's the last we'll see of Mr. Principles."

"I'll pray for him."

"You do that," Glenn said ruefully as he stood to leave.

As Glenn walked down the wide corridor leading away from the pastor's study, he passed Megan who was coming to see her father.

"Hello young lady, congratulations on your recent coming of age. That was quite a celebration your family gave you. Thanks for the invitation," Glenn said in an attempt to be friendly.

"Thanks, but I don't remember you being on the guest list," she said coldly and kept walking. Megan had overheard her father talk about Glenn in very derogatory terms and had formed a bad attitude toward him. She didn't like him even though she barely knew him.

Glenn did his best to hide the hurt she inflicted and committed himself to praying for her.

The pastor's secretary was on the telephone and waved to Megan as she approached. Megan lightly tapped on her father's office door.

"Come in," said a voice from within. Pastor T.J. stood as Megan entered.

"Hello honey, what brings you here in the middle of the day?"

"I wanted to get your opinion."

"Oh? My opinion on what?"

"I want to know what you think about me getting a job. Now that I'm a big girl, I kinda wanted to move on with my life."

"A job? Where? There's nothing in this town but minimum wage jobs and you are much too good for them. How about I make a few calls and see if I can't get you something in New York or Washington, D.C.? I've got connections and could get you a high paying job doing whatever you like."

"No daddy, I like it here and was thinking about getting a job at the local newspaper. I heard that they have an opening."

"Yes, they have an opening all right. They fired that hotshot reporter over some technicality. I understand the editor is a tough guy to work for too."

"Yes I've met him once or twice when I went down there to see Chase, that hotshot reporter, as you called him."

"Why did you go there Megan?"

"Remember? I was in the Journalism club at college? I went there a couple of times to get some help writing an article. That's when I met Mr. Berkowitz."

"Well if you think you can handle the pressure of that kind of work, go for it. It might be fun," he said, though not convinced.

CHAPTER 7

Maxine's Diner

Chase didn't notice when the older gentleman entered the diner, but he looked up and smiled as he approached his table. "May I join you?" The older man softly said. Chase nodded.

Maxine's Diner was a common place for the local people to catch up on the events of the day, swap fishing stories, and get a good meal. For Chase, it was the closest thing to a home-cooked meal. This was the second time he stopped by there that day, and he'd probably stop there one more time after work. The place was crowded with county linemen, firemen, and a few deputies. Seating was limited, so Glenn headed to the first empty spot he could find.

The waitress came over. "Want some coffee, Glenn?"

"Yes, please ... black," Glenn said and took a seat across from Chase. The day had been cool and sunny, and Glenn was returning from a very successful fishing trip with his friend John.

Chase pointed to his cup. "Could I get a warm up?...*Please!*" Chase repeated, looking at Glenn. "That's a word I haven't heard in a while. You'd think that all these new folks would be grateful for the town opening its arms to them. In most parts of the country they'd be unwelcome, especially during these hard times."

"My friend John isn't complaining whether they say please or not as long as they say thank you with a great big, fat commission check at closing."

"I've noticed that his land development company has been doing a...pardon the pun...a 'land office business.'"

"Yes, he's doing rather well for himself, even if he's semi-retired. Say, aren't you the reporter who just got fired from the Observer? I understand ole Stan isn't the easiest to work for."

"Yeah, he's like a cross between a skunk and a porcupine, but really if you get on his *good side* he's a pussy cat...it's just getting there's the problem. Didn't I see you at that Q and A service the other night?"

"It's called a praise and worship service," Glenn gently explained.

"Well, it seemed more like a Q and A class I took in college." Chase paused before changing topics. "Say, this whole free speech and morality thing has got me thinking; maybe it's time for me to rethink my thinking. Maybe it's time I started back to church. My dad, when he was alive, was a part-time preacher back in the North Carolina hills. I can still hear him hollering 'Amen' to the rhythm of the guest preachers that would come to fill in. And before my mom passed away, you should have heard her sing, or try to sing. That was a trip."

"Now, don't you go speakin' ill of the dead. My wife, God rest her soul, was a godly woman. She loved to sing." He smiled at the memories. Glenn paused to sip his coffee. "Son, now I know you didn't ask me to stop by here to reminisce over your parents. What's on your mind?"

"Glenn … may I call you Glenn?"

The older gentleman nodded.

"Glenn, maybe I got this all wrong, but I felt a kindred spirit with you a few weeks ago. Something told me that you *see* things, you *hear* things … you *know* things! I have a hunch that not all is well in Paradise."

Glenn pushed his coffee cup back and leaned in closer. "Son, let's take a walk."

The Beaumont Observer

Stan looked up as Megan stepped into the Observer.

"Well what can I do for you, young lady?"

"Good morning to you too, Mr. Berkowitz. I'm here to apply for the opening you have for a reporter," she said without apology.

"I didn't know I was hiring."

"Didn't you have a reporter a few days ago?"

"Well yes."

"And do you have one now?"

"No, not exactly"

"Well either you do or you don't, and according to the newspaper, you don't!

That's, of course, if you can believe everything that you read in the newspaper."

Stan liked her feisty spirit and stood rubbing his chin.

"Okay, I got an opening, you can use Chase's old office, but along with the office comes the responsibility. His was the current events column. Do you think you can handle it?"

"I was a reporter with the junior college's Journalism club and know something about writing current events."

"Well you are in the big league now, young lady, and you've got a dead-line in five days, so get to work. I need something on my desk by Friday, you got that?"

"Yes sir, and thanks."

"It's Stan to you and don't thank me yet. I haven't read your first article," he said as he walked back to his office.

CHAPTER 8

The Community First Church

Chase began attending the Saturday evening Praise and Worship services regularly, much to the delight of Megan. He even got an invitation to the preacher's house for Sunday dinner if he would come on a Sunday morning. The thought of a real home-cooked meal was very tempting. Megan even talked him into signing a request for membership card, and that he be taken under review for membership.

Membership in the Community First Church now required a financial and a criminal background check. Plus, they required that you signed a Church Covenant. The new Church Covenant read like a contract: lots of legalese, lots of whereofs and wherefors. The bottom line was that if Chase signed on to this, he was in for a wild ride down a dark road.

Chase signed the Covenant.

Within a few weeks Chase was asked to come in for an interview with the Membership Committee. Nervously he entered the lobby and passed Perks. No one was there at the time, or he would have gotten a cup of coffee to calm his jitters. He approached the receptionist's desk and cleared his throat.

The receptionist looked up from a book that she was reading, a book written by Pastor T.J., entitled, *Growing the Church from the Outside.*

"Hi, I'm—" Chase was interrupted by the receptionist.

"Yes, I know who you are, and the committee is expecting you." With that she stood up and led Chase down the well-lit hallway of the newly built Baxter Administrative Wing. It was dedicated to one of the former members, now deceased; the dear Ms. Emma Baxter. The receptionist was smartly dressed. *None of this casual attire here,* he thought. She grabbed the handle of the large oak door before Chase could and swung it open. The room was occupied in the center with a large glass-covered table. The table reminded him of the dean of journalism's office back at UNC, only this one was larger. Around the table sat a number of rather stoic looking individuals. At the head of the table sat Pastor T.J. Richards. He was dressed in a three-button suit, with a tie that was designed to make a statement. The statement was very clear. Power.

The interview began with the usual preliminary statements about not being nervous. It didn't work. Then as if on cue each member of the committee asked Chase a question. Chase wasn't sure if the purpose of this interview was to get him into the membership of the church or to keep him out.

"Have you read the Constitution and Bylaws?" one member asked.

"Do you agree with the Constitution and Bylaws?" another asked as a follow-up.

"I have read both the Constitution and the Bylaws and have signed them," Chase said, avoiding telling a lie. He was in church after all.

"We have reviewed your financial statement," said one committee member, "and frankly we have some concerns. How do you propose supporting the budget of Community First Church?"

"Well, I have a college degree and I am looking for a job in the professional job market," Chase said respectfully.

"Yes, well, I see here that your training was in journalism. Are you a journalist?"

"No, sir! I have had it with that bunch, and they have had it with me. We parted company under rather tenuous circumstances."

That was only half true, but who's counting? Chase thought to himself.

"Have you ever been arrested or bonded?" The last interrogator asked.

"No, sir! I've got a clean record."

They knew that answer before they asked it, but just wanted to see his reaction.

Then the pastor spoke. "Well, men, I see no reason why we should not let Mr. Uuh," T.J. looked down at his notes. "Mr. Newton come into the fold." Then turning to

Chase, "Mr. Newton, we will take this under review and let you know as soon as possible. It would help us make the decision sooner if we were informed that you have been gainfully employed. We are not wanting to have any undue stress put upon our benevolence budget by letting the unemployed or underemployed join our ranks."

With that he stood, as did his underlings, leaving Chase to take his cue from them. He rose to his feet, and the pastor, followed by his entourage, quietly slipped through a paneled door that Chase had not noticed before.

He stood there for a moment or two until he heard someone clearing her throat. It was the receptionist.

"You are dismissed, please follow me." With that she turned and briskly walked back to the lobby and pushed the button to let Chase exit the front door.

Within a week of Chase getting his job at the First National Bank of Beaumont, he received an official-looking letter in the mail informing him that he was a member in good standing of the Community First Church. He was assigned an elder and a deacon. Fortunately his deacon was none other than Glenn Tibbits, and his dear friend, John Wiener, was his elder. Also, with the membership letter came a box of numbered tithe envelopes. They were about as subtle as a hand grenade.

John Wiener, his new elder, was a recent newcomer himself, predating the pastor by a few years. His land development company was doing quite well considering the economic down times that the rest of the country was in. He joined the struggling First Church, and with his generous giving, ingratiated himself with the membership, especially with Glenn who at the time was the adjunct treasurer. John, a real estate attorney and developer had the freedom of travel and time for an occasional fishing trip with his friend Glenn, a retired jeweler. Both men were financially set, and both were widowers, but John had his eye set on the widow Ann Conley. It was John who brought in the new Wal-Mart, along with developing a large tract of land west of town. The houses he was building ran in the $300,000's and were selling like hotcakes. Most of the buyers were these newcomers from back east. At least that's the way it looked if you noticed the old license plates.

Ann Conley was another new resident, and John happened to be the closing attorney for the purchase of her new palatial home she purchased overlooking the town. Who the builder was isn't known. It somehow was never put into the public records. As a matter of fact, John was responsible for helping a lot of folks find housing, though not always built by his construction company.

That was another thing that puzzled Chase. It seemed that with the influx of new residents also came the expansion of Community First Church. *Could it be the pas-*

tor's teaching? The Praise and Worship services? Or the new name? What was drawing so many people to that church and not any of the other churches in the area? Chase put these questions down in his notebook to be answered later. In the meantime he needed to focus his energies on getting some quality time getting to know Megan better. *Maybe, just maybe, he might get that home-cooked meal,* he thought.

"Hi M," Chase said as he met Megan in front of Perks. It was Saturday night and the Praise and Worship service was just getting started.

"Well hey stranger," Megan replied, "do you want to get some coffee before we go in?"

"Yeah sure, why not. I understand you got my old job," said Chase as they took a seat at one of the tables.

"That's right and your office was a mess."

"Yeah, well I kinda left in a hurry you might say."

"Well Stan was a bit reluctant to hire me, but I convinced him that he needed me."

"Oh really? How did you do that?"

"Mr. Berkowitz, Stan, likes a straight shooter and I just told him he had an opening and that I could handle the job, so he hired me on the spot."

"That's great M. Did you get your first article in on time?"

"Yep! Right on time and he liked it," she said smugly.

"Sweet! What was it about?"

"I wrote about the bank."

"The bank?"

"Yep, you know First National Bank."

"Yeah I know which bank, but what could you possibly write about a bank?"

"Well the article head line says it all, it reads; How Safe is the First National Bank?"

"Great lead M! What did you find? If I may ask."

"I did some research on the bank. Although it is a pillar of stability in the region now, the old three-story brick building has been robbed once."

"It was?" Chase asked with surprise.

"Yep! It was built back in 1883 when the railroad came through, but in 1889, Butch Cassidy and the Sundance Kid robbed it. Back then they used a nearby canyon named Robber's Roost, as their hide out."

"Robber's Roost is not far from Beaumont," Chase said incredulously.

"Yes I know, I included some back ground information about Robber's Roost as well. It seems that it was a popular outlaw hideout for over thirty years during the late 1800's. It is located within the Grand Canyon along the Outlaw Trail in southeastern Utah. Butch Cassidy, a Circleville, Utah, native, was the grandson of a Mormon handcart pioneer. His original name was Robert Leroy Parker, but he changed his name to Butch Cassidy. He began using the Roost in the 1880s to hide cattle that he rustled and considered it an ideal hideout due to the many lookout points. That particular area is sandwiched between the Colorado River, Green River, and Dirty Devil River. The Wild Bunch used it after a Colorado bank robbery in 1889."

"Well it sounds like you are off to a great start with your first article, M. I'm glad Stan liked it. By the way, is the bank safe?"

"Yes. That's what I plan on writing about next week."

"I sure hope so, since that's where I work," he said as they entered the auditorium.

CHAPTER 9

First National Bank of Beaumont

Ever since his recent stand on the free speech issue, Chase seemed to have picked up a number of friends in high places: the former mayor of Beaumont; an elder at Community First Church; the bank president and deacon at Community First Church; and the fire chief and chairmen of the deacon board at none other than Community First Church. It may be of interest to point out that the bank president and deacon at Community First Church was actually a deaconess. Her name was Ann Conley.

This incestuous relationship with the new residents and the church was a bit alarming to both Glenn and Chase. Both saw it, and both kept it to themselves.

With the friendship of his newfound friends, Chase found getting a job at the First National Bank of Beaumont to be easier than he had expected. He made the assumption that his deacon may have been responsible for his new employment. But how or what strings were pulled he had no clue. What better way to get the inside scoop on a church than to follow the money, or in this case, find its source.

As chief loan officer, Chase now had access to accounts and background information of nearly everyone in town. The only problem was accessing it without raising the attention of the ever-watchful Ann Conley. It seemed that Ann had taken a particular liking to Chase. Not just over the free speech issue, but there was something else that he couldn't put his finger on. It couldn't be his good looks. He was indeed a good-looking young man of twenty-five. His sandy blond hair, blue eyes, and muscular build (kept up by running five miles every morning) may have been one factor. Surely that wouldn't attract a thirty-five-year-old widow, would it?

Ann, or Ms. C., as she insisted being called, was no slouch when it came to looks as well. It was obvious that she understood that fact and used it to her advantage. She was rather tall for a woman, and well built and she carried herself as a woman with poise and class.

She was used to getting her way.

With the job issue resolved, Chase now could focus his attention on phase two: winning Megan's confidence. If he could make good on the dinner invitation he just might get a glimpse behind the veil of secrecy surrounding the Richards' home. He needed a way in and that seemed the quickest way.

Little did he know that there were other forces at work.

One day as Chase sat at his desk working on the latest loan application, Susan Bailes stepped into his office unannounced. Susan Bailes was a bank examiner. Her job was to find any irregularities or discrepancies. To most in the banking industry, the bank examiner was the scourge of society, but her auburn hair and cool green eyes didn't strike Chase as any scourge. Rather, her feminine build and southern drawl all but left Chase as a stammering junior high kid. Chase was hopelessly, irreparably smitten. He was doomed to spend countless hours going over meaningless numbers with this gorgeous woman, and that without a word of complaint.

This new development not only complicated his plans for Megan, but it also gave him a perfect excuse to open the books of countless new residents without the prying eyes of Ms. C., who was getting more overt with her interest.

Chase had a problem. *How does one keep the unwanted advances of one's boss at bay, and nurture a relationship with the preacher's daughter, and keep one's thinking straight every time Susan Bailes walked into the room? he thought to himself.*

His was a position not to be envied.

But envied it was!

CHAPTER 10

The First National Bank

Every time Chase logged on to his computer, not only was Ms. C. watching, but also Jimmy Stevens. Jimmy Stevens had worked at the bank since high school. He had worked his way up the ladder and should have been given the chief loan officer position; it was *his* position and it didn't set well with him that he was passed over. His beef was as much with Ms. C. as it was with Chase.

Someone had to pay, but whom? And then who would pay next? Jimmy thought as he watched his computer screen.

Jimmy was forever looking out for Jimmy. He had a way of sticking his nose in where it was not wanted. He would have made a great investigative reporter. Chase thought about recommending him for his old job. He would have if he thought that he might not get it back.

Chase's big break came as he noticed the frequent visits by John Wiener to the bank. It wasn't that he was there on business. He was there to see Ms. C. Sometimes his visits would include lunch, which would last for hours. Word had it that they were having an affair, but that was just speculation. With the absence of Ann from the picture, Chase and Susan felt at liberty to open and examine as many accounts as time would allow.

The examination was thorough and quite revealing. It seemed that many new residents were not who they claimed to be. Much of the funding came from sources outside the U.S., from places like Jordan, Yemen, and Turkey. The sources were nearly untraceable! Nearly, but with time and a little help from the outside, the sources could be discovered.

But was there time?

Jimmy was already causing some troubles for Chase's investigation. One time he walked into the room and saw Susan perched on the corner of Chase's desk doing a background check on a number of key leaders of the Community First Church.

"What are you doing checking up on these people? Don't you know that it's against the law to be prying into people's private financial records?"

Susan's southern accent suddenly evaporated as she spun around and pierced him with those green eyes. "I have every right to examine whoever I please, whenever I please. I have the backing of the State and the Federal Government. And it's none of your business who I investigate. Maybe the next background check will be yours. Got anything to hide?"

Jimmy stomped out, but neither Chase nor Susan thought that was the end of it. *We'll have to keep an eye on him*, Susan thought.

The next day was Friday and Jimmy was in Ms. C.'s office complaining that Susan's examination was getting out of hand. His motivation wasn't so much to get Susan in trouble as much as it was to help his own position in the bank. Of course, the bank president dared not interfere with the bank examiner; that would raise all sorts of red flags, and that was not what Ms. C. needed right now.

While Jimmy was in her office, he kept one eye on Ms. C and the other on her computer screen. It was then, while he was talking to her, that events took an unexpected turn.

A very important document lay open on her desk as she was reading it over. Just about that time, John sashayed into her office. "Want to go for a ride in my new BMW? Look it's Friday, why don't you take the rest of the day off and we'll go someplace?"

John's new BMW 330Ci was certainly a luxury vehicle. It was a jet-black convertible, complete with leather seats, mag wheels, six-disc CD player, iPod® interface, GPS, and BMW ULF hands free phone system with Bluetooth. "With the new technology in suspension, the car rides like a dream" he said, ignoring Jimmy.

As a matter of fact, he didn't even notice his presence. Neither did Ms. C. as she grabbed her purse and left without so much as a good-bye. Jimmy stood there in the now empty office of Ms. C. He noticed a very impressive document lying on her desk, and stepped around it to get a closer look. Curiosity kills the cat, they say. It certainly drove Jimmy to make a snap decision. He recognized this document to be of immeasurable importance, and so he quietly slipped it under his sports coat and left the bank, and headed off to his apartment. Sitting in his one-room apartment, Jimmy suddenly realized that he was now the new power broker in town.

But time was not on his side!

When Ms. C. returned to the bank to lock up, she discovered that the document was missing! Where could it have gone? Who could have taken it? she thought. She picked up the phone and made a call

"John, I've got a problem."

Chase and Susan decided to return to the bank after hours on Friday to do some more digging. That's when they hit pay dirt.

"Chase, would you look at this?" Susan said as she rotated her laptop around for him to see. "I not only discovered the fraudulent backgrounds of most newcomers in town, but one newcomer stands out above the rest. Pastor T.J. Richards is definitely not who he claims to be."

Chase rose from his chair to get a better look.

She continued, "Not only was T.J. educated at Bruton College, he was trained by the Imaam Ahmed Abdul Nudobie, an outspoken Muslim cleric. For years he was a member of the AMS. The Association of Muslim Scholars is a group of Sunni scholars. Many of its members favor the Hanbali School of fiqh law over the Hanafi School, which has traditionally been dominant in Iraq.

Imaam Ahmed Abdul Nudobie has a history of anti-American rhetoric, but with age, he has tempered his views. Nudobie told a Houston audience "he was blessed to live in a country that is stable and safe, and in which he has thrived."

Chase opened the box of pizza that the delivery boy just brought and grabbed a piece. "Want some?"

"Yeah, I'm starved!" She continued in between bites. "Oh, he did attend Bruton College," she continued, "and did graduate with a divinity degree, but his major was in Eastern Religions. His studies led him to sit under such renown Hindu clerics as the Dalai Lama and Tenzin Gyatso."

"He eventually found that yoga and meditation were far more rewarding than his liberal college's Bible studies," Chase surmised.

"Yeah, and as a matter of fact, the dean of religious studies encouraged young T.J. to gain as much wisdom as possible from the masters. A quick background check of Dean Wilson shows that he himself was a grand master, being a deeply committed agnostic. He, too, had long exposed his mind to meditation, drug-induced trances, out-of-body experiences, and spirit guides. It was through Dean Wilson that T.J. was introduced to the now infamous Imaam Ahmed Abdul Nudobie. It was Dean Wilson who mentored T.J. Richards into the man that he is today, or at least the man he appears to be. And it was Dean Wilson who recommended T.J. to my father for consideration for the pastorate of the "First Church.""

Chase looked at Susan, "Glenn Tibbits is your father?"

"Yeah, long story. Sometime I'll tell you about it. But for now we need to inform the authorities."

"Well, let's keep digging; it's amazing what you can find on the Internet just by typing in a few names and key words. Maybe we can get to the source of the money," Chase said enthusiastically.

Susan entered the name "Estella Richards" into the search engine and waited a moment.

"Hey, look at this: Mrs. Richards is an ambassador's daughter, born and educated in Yemen. She speaks three languages," she said.

Having been raised in the Middle East, Estella had an affinity for the people. It comes as no surprise that her loyalty for the U.S was fragile at best.

"Look here," she said as she scrolled down further, "it says that Dean Wilson was the one who arranged for the first meeting between T.J. and Estella. After a brief romance they got married. Dean Wilson performed the ceremony."

"Looks like a marriage made in heaven."

"Or worse!" Susan said as she grabbed the last slice of cold pizza. "The Dean, as he likes to be called, retired from an organization called 'The Order.'"

"Let me do a search of The Order and you keep working on the financial angle."

Chase entered "The Order," and hit pay dirt. "You gotta see this. It looks like we got us a major conspiracy going on right under our noses. This so-called 'The Order' has tentacles all over the place. There are major players all over the Middle East and in our government as well as places of higher learning. This thing is huge! And T.J. sits at the Head of the Table of The Order."

"The Order," Chase continued, "is a multi-national, quasi-religious consortium of nation builders or nation re-builders. They have been in existence as far back as the Crusaders. They have been at war with any form of commercialism, free enterprise, and Christianity. Their goal is to create the perfect society, one void of Christians and Jews. They tried and failed over the centuries in countries such as Prussia by overthrowing the Czar; in France, by causing the French Revolution; in Spain, during the Spanish Inquisition; and even in the American Revolution, and the War of 1812. The Order backed the Southern Confederacy and Napoleon Bonaparte. Before WWI, members of The Order controlled Germany, which also prepared the way for Hitler's rise to power preceding WWII. Their ultimate goal is to establish their own land base and to form their own nation. From that base they would launch an aggressive expansion program. They would use either political subterfuge or open war to accomplish their evil purpose of world domination."

"The Dean wouldn't appreciate it if he knew what we know," Susan mused.

"Well, we can't let that happen now can we," Chase said as he ran his hand though his hair.

"We need to let the authorities know before this thing gets out of control. I'm heading to Denver tonight," Susan said as she began gathering her belongings.

"Why not pick up the phone and call your boss in the morning?"

"Too risky. They might have the phones bugged. I'm heading out now; maybe I can get there and be waiting with all this information when my boss gets to the office."

"So who is your boss and how can he help us?" Chase said with concern in his voice.

"Look, this thing is bigger than we can handle, and the people I know are the only ones who can do anything about it. Why don't you see if you can make good on the Sunday dinner promise and see if you can't learn something."

"Great, get a home-cooked meal right before I get shot."

"Don't be so morbid. I don't see where it says these people are violent," Susan said.

"You don't get this much power without knocking a few heads around."

The printer dutifully printed out the information, and Susan stuffed it in her briefcase. Chase reached down and squeezed her hand.

"You be careful driving, it's been raining all night and the roads can be pretty treacherous going through those mountain passes. It being Friday night, there are some crazy people out there."

"Don't worry, I've driven them plenty of times visiting Dad."

"Susan, you gotta tell me more about that when you get back. How about over dinner?"

"That sounds great. I'll see you in a few days."

Susan slipped out the back door of the bank and into the night. She didn't notice the black sedan parked in the adjoining parking lot. Neither did she think much about it when a set of headlights appeared in her rearview mirror. It was too late to think about it when the car behind her pulled a PIT maneuver.

The PIT maneuver is a method by which one car pursuing another can force the car in front to abruptly turn, causing the driver to lose control and stop. The acronym PIT is Precision Immobilization Technique. The PIT begins when the pursuing vehicle pulls alongside the car ahead so that his right front fender is aligned with the left rear fender of the car in front. The car in the rear gently makes contact with the front car's rear fender and then steers sharply to the right. As soon as the car's rear tires lose traction it starts to go into a spin. This is exactly what happened. Before Susan could react her car went into and over the guardrail. No one heard her car hit the bottom of the canyon. But someone watched it happen.

Glenn woke up in the small hours with a sense of urgency to pray, and pray hard. So he took his old tattered Bible and went to his study and opened it to his favorite verse, "And all things, whatsoever ye shall ask in prayer, believing, ye shall receive," Matthew 21:22 (KJV).

He claimed the promises as he prayed earnestly for Susan's safety and protection, and for his pastor and church leadership that God would do a work in their hearts. Then he turned his attention on Chase. He had a feeling that Chase was searching for the truth. *If only the Lord would*

open the eyes of his understanding and reveal the truth to him, he was sure that Chase would accept it, Glenn thought as he gently closed his Bible.

He prayed till the sun was well above the horizon.

CHAPTER II

Jimmy's Apartment

Both Jimmy and Ms. C. were in difficult positions. For Ms. C., the fact that she lost the document meant disaster. *Who took it? Who had it? What were they planning to do with it?* she wondered.

Time was running out!

The annual conference of The Order was to convene the following week on October thirty-first, the Day of Consummation, as they called it. Then, the document would be ratified, and The Order would take its rightful place in the community of nations.

Jimmy's dilemma was quite different.

He sat in his one-room apartment with the title deed to half of the United States. *Was this real? How could such a document exist? Wasn't the United States of America a sov-*

ereign nation? How could this have happened? Someone got sloppy or greedy… or both! But how do you broker a deal with a document of such magnitude… and live? Jimmy mused as he stuffed the pages into an envelope.

Time was running out for Jimmy, too!

It wouldn't be long before Ms. C. figured out who took the document. Should I go to her and try to cut a deal? Get a cut of the action? Or should I go to the next level? This was indeed America. This was the land of free enterprise. Or should I go to the authorities? I couldn't just sit idly by and watch my country be sold to foreign interests. But to whom do I go? Who can I trust? Not Ms. C. and not her Romeo boyfriend John.

Just then his cell phone vibrated. *Should I answer it? The number was not familiar,* Jimmy thought as he stared at the caller ID. *Who would be calling me in the middle of the night anyway?* He reluctantly flipped his phone open.

"Hello?" Jimmy said.

"Jimmy, this is Chase."

He let out a sigh of relief. "Yeah, what are *you doing* calling me in the middle of the night? Don't you sleep?"

"Jimmy, just listen to me; we've discovered some really important stuff about the new people in town, including the pastor of the Community First Church."

"I'm listening."

And so was someone else! A highly sophisticated listening device; "a bug" began picking up every word that was being said and digitally recording it.

Someone else knew! But who?

CHAPTER 12

The City Jail

Sheriff Conyers was a long-time resident of Beaumont. His dad claimed that he was with one of the posses who chased Butch Cassidy all the way to Robber's Roost and participated in a gunfight with the Wild Bunch. Of course that was all bravado, but it sounded good when told by the old-timers at Maxine's Diner. He worked his way up from a rookie cop on the downtown strip to now, twenty years later, the well-connected chief of police. He had lots of friends in high places and some in not so high places as well. "You don't get to my position and stay there without information," he often said. And for that, he needed someone to do his legwork.

Enter Luke Cooley! Luke Cooley was a high school dropout with a growing rap sheet. His father, now deceased, was Sheriff Conyers best friend and deputy. Deputy Cooley was killed in the line of duty. He left behind a grieving wife and teenaged son who didn't take his loss very well. He dropped out of high school in his senior year and learned the art of stealing cars. It seemed at the time there was a hot market for certain makes of cars and the chop shop on Lucky Street was the place to take them. Only Lucky Street wasn't so lucky. A former economic center now was a row of run-down buildings, most of which were vacant. The windows of the houses were either boarded up or broken out. One night Sheriff Conyers and his men showed up. They netted the usual brand of common thieves, among them Luke Cooley. Luke was never that motivated. His priorities revolved around three things: sleeping, drinking, or cavorting.

"Luke," said Sheriff Conyers, "I should arrest you, but to honor your father, I'm going to offer you a job. This would not only serve to keep an eye on you, but also provide me with a person to do the unpleasant tasks."

As it turned out, Luke was quite good at doing bad things. A number of unwanted persons were quietly dispatched. The town suddenly got the reputation for being a good place to raise a family. All this coincided with the upcoming elections, and Sheriff Conyers wanted very badly to win re-election. As a way to guarantee that victory, he needed information. It wasn't unusual for the good sheriff to do some eavesdropping.

"You never know where you might learn something," he said to Luke.

And Sheriff Conyers was always eager to learn!

CHAPTER 13

On the edge of a cliff

The car Susan was driving went careening out of control, hit the guardrail and flipped. There was silence, then there was the sound of crashing, then there was silence.

Susan woke to the sound of dripping. *What is that sound I'm hearing? What is that smell?* She thought to herself. She felt nauseous and light-headed. Her ears were ringing. *What is that smell?* The car's air bags all deployed at the same time cushioning most of the impact. But the fall crushed the car around her; she couldn't move her legs, they were pinned and the pain in her shoulder was excruciating. She felt herself going into shock. *What is that smell?* She realized that what she was hearing and smelling was gasoline, and it was dripping on her. In that moment Susan realized that she was about to die, and she prayed, *Lord Jesus, I know I'm ready to meet you and I am not afraid, but I believe that you gave me a job to do and I haven't finished it. Help me, please!* At that moment the peace of God that passes understanding flooded her heart and she relaxed waiting for the end to come.

That part of the canyon was very steep, some three hundred feet to the bottom; however, there was a ledge about thirty feet just down from the edge of the road. Susan's car had hit that ledge and crashed the front of the car into the passenger's compartment. There it sat perched on the edge, waiting to slip off and fall to the bottom.

A face suddenly appeared through the broken windshield. "Lady, are you all right?" It was Sheriff Conyers. He had watched the whole thing unfold, but was helpless to stop it.

"I can't move my legs, I think they're crushed between the dashboard and the seat. I feel sick."

The Sheriff reached in and felt Susan's face. "You're going into shock. I gotta get you out of there and fast." With that he reached his powerful forearm in and ripped part of the dashboard away from Susan's legs. Within minutes he had her legs free and was pulling her out. "You smell like gas."

"I know this car is going to blow any minute," Susan said as the sheriff pulled her free. Susan did have the presence of mind to grab her briefcase. As she lay there on the rocky ledge the car slipped and fell crashing to the bottom of the canyon and exploding into a large fireball.

"Man, that was close," the sheriff said as he returned with a blanket to keep her from going into shock. "I gotta call this in."

It took the ambulance crew thirty minutes to hoist Susan up the steep side of the canyon. She was life-flighted to the nearest hospital.

"Sheriff, God sent you by just in time. I thought I was a goner."

"I was monitoring the phone conversation between Chase and Jimmy, when I noticed a car followed you out of the bank parking lot. I got a look at the license plate of the sedan and was calling it in when he pulled that PIT maneuver. There are only a few in this county who would know how to do that, and I have a pretty good idea who."

Earlier in the year, Sheriff Conyers had taken Luke out to the police academy's driving range and taught him how to perform the PIT maneuver. It looked as if he was a good student!

The paramedics had given Susan something for the pain, and she was fading fast.

"Sheriff, my briefcase ..." Her voice weakened.

"I got it, hon—whatever's in it is safe with me. I'll see you in the hospital."

With that the helicopter rose and headed off to Mercy Hospital with Susan's broken body. The helicopter touched down on the helipad as a medical team rushed to its bay door. The gurney was readied, and Susan was transferred to it along with several IV bags feeding her critical life-sustaining fluids. Mercy Hospital, though small, was equipped with a class one triage unit. It was the main medical facility for receiving injured skiers and mountain climbers. And with the recent fires sparked by the Santa Anna winds it had its share of injured fire fighters as well. All in all, Susan was in good hands. There happened to be a specialist for internal injuries on duty that night.

"By rights you should be dead," the ER doctor said as Susan blinked away the drug-induced sleep.

"I think that was their goal."

"You took a pretty bad fall and you have multiple internal injuries along with a broken leg and a displaced left shoulder."

"You mean to say that I'm done with ballroom dancing for the foreseeable future?"

"You're lucky to have a future, but I'm fairly certain that in time you'll make a full recovery."

"I don't have time, I was carrying some very important documents and I need to speak to my boss ASAP."

"Okay, we'll get you patched up and into a room and after some sleep you can call the FBI if you like."

"How did you know that I was going to call the FBI?"

"I didn't, I was just kidding."

Just then Sheriff Conyers came rushing into the ER.

"Is she gonna make it?"

"Yes, but no ballroom dancing for a few months."

"I am placing her under protective custody; she has vital information and is now a state witness. Her identity must remain a secret. Those who tried to kill her just might try again if they ever learn that she survived the crash."

"In that case, I can file a report that she was DOA, dead-on-arrival. By rights she should have been."

"God is not finished with me just yet," Susan sited.

"Well, we're not finished with you yet either, so you lay back, and let us do some repair work."

"Doc, give me a minute alone with my witness. Susan, do you have any idea why they were following you and why they wanted to kill you?"

"Believe me, you don't want to know."

"I already know enough to get myself killed, I might as well learn the rest."

"Sheriff, take a look inside my briefcase and you'll have all the answers you need.

With that, the orderly wheeled Susan off to surgery.

The bug planted in Jimmy's apartment was not the only listening device involved. It seemed that Glenn Tibbits had taken an interest in technology as well. Only he didn't need a bug or a Luke. He just needed to be standing close to Chase. As a matter of fact, he was in the same room with Chase running the digital recorder. Little did either of them know the powder keg that Jimmy was sitting on.

But they were about to find out!

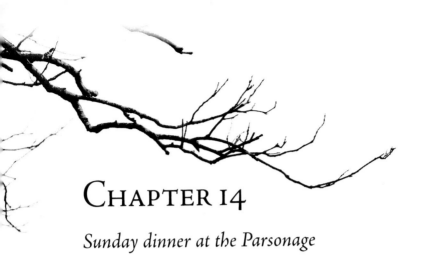

CHAPTER 14

Sunday dinner at the Parsonage

"Man, am I hungry. I can't wait for some home-cooked food. Does your mom do all the cooking around your house?" Chase asked Megan as she drove her black SUV back from the Sunday morning church service.

Before she could answer, Chase looked around the vehicle and said, "I seem to remember seeing this SUV a few months ago."

"Oh, really?"

"Yeah, whoever was driving it nearly ran me over as I was crossing the street."

"It was probably my dad," she said coyly.

"Yeah, right," Chase dropped the subject not wanting to cause hard feelings right before he had his first home-cooked meal in ... longer than he could remember.

"Getting back to your first question, Mom doesn't do any of the cooking around our house. We have a cook who does all that. Actually, she's a nutritionist; everything she makes is good for you."

"I sure hope I like it."

"Oh, you will. I hope you don't mind sitting in the guest dining room. We have other guests coming for dinner besides you."

"Oh, who are they?"

"I don't know, just a bunch of very important people. Some wearing turbans, some wearing suits, some wearing a burqa, the traditional head coverings. Fortunately Mom speaks three languages and she can interpret if you want to say 'hi' to anyone."

"I probably won't be saying 'hi' to anybody besides your dad. By the way, do I call him Pastor, Reverend, Father, what?"

"I don't know, just call him T.J. That's what he prefers."

"Somehow I don't think that all those muckity-mucks will be calling him T.J."

Megan parked her SUV, and they got out and started walking up the flagstone walkway leading to the house. Actually it wasn't a house as one might have imagined. This was a cross between a mansion and a conference center. It could have been a second White House.

"Look at the size of this place. Do you actually live here?"

"Yes, silly, we've always lived in nice homes."

"This ain't no home that I've ever seen."

"It's just 'home sweet home' to me. Come in, and I'll show you around before all the other guests arrive."

They toured the palatial home with Megan pointing out some of the more outstanding artwork and sculptures.

Some were rather embarrassing to look at in mixed company, so Chase moved ahead quickly. Megan, acting as a tour guide, showed Chase the fitness center and spa, the game room, the entertainment room, complete with theater seating and surround sound, and the library. These rooms occupied the lower level and were accessed by an elevator. The main level featured the living room, dining rooms, kitchen, and sunroom. The living room was an eclectic collection of old world and post-modern design. Couches and love seats were placed around the spacious room in conversational arrangements. The sunroom combined the idea of bringing the outdoors in, and the indoors out, with lush foliage strategically located throughout the area. The upper floor was the residential section and also housed the conference center. That was off limits except for immediate family and guests. Megan did say that there were seven large bedroom suites each having their own bathroom, and that the elevator leading to the upper level needed a security code to enter.

Sitting in the guest overflow dining room wasn't that bad. Chase was keeping Megan company. Between her chatter and the interruptions of the servers asking him if he wanted bleu cheese or ranch dressing, sweet tea or sun tea, ham or turkey, he was barely able to follow the conversations going on in the other room. Although they weren't discussing any major business, they were excited about something about to happen on Friday. One time he heard the word *consummation* before there was a lot of shushing. Then it got quiet and the conversation moved on to sports and the like. Chase had picked up on one thing; he hoped that Susan would be back soon, and they could act before Friday.

She didn't return.

With the annual conference of The Order scheduled for the end of the week, already guests were arriving. Ms. C. was frantic. Finding, retrieving, and silencing that person or persons who took the document was job number one. She needed an edge; she needed someone in the know, someone who could do her dirty work. The name Luke Cooley had come up a few times in the city planners meetings. Not that he was of any interest to her back then, but this was now—this was an emergency. Earlier in the week she had used Sheriff Conyers' cell phone and had pulled Luke's cell number off of the sheriff's phone in the event that she might need it.

Today was that day.

She had already called his number once with a job for him to do. Now she needed him again. She picked up her cell phone and dialed the number. It rang.

"Luke? Did you finish the job I gave you last night?"

"Yep, went smooth as silk. No witnesses! It'll go down as a weather-related accident."

"Good, listen very carefully, I have another job for you to do."

CHAPTER 15

Jimmy's Apartment

Jimmy, frankly, wasn't impressed with the tone of Ms. C.'s voice, especially at two o'clock in the morning. Yes, she was desperate; yes, she was insistent; and yes, she was fishing. But Jimmy hadn't bitten. With the information he had acquired from Chase, he was now in the position where he could have some power.

Real power!

The problem Jimmy had was finding a buyer, and he needed to find one fast. Ms. C. indicated that she was under a lot of pressure and she needed to have a problem solved before the end of the week.

Jimmy couldn't go to the Chinese. They were some of the ones providing the funding. He couldn't go to the U.S. They were the ones selling off its assets. Ever since the economic downturn, as they were calling it (really it was just an old-fashioned depression), large tracts of land were being foreclosed. The problem was that those large tracts of land happened to be called Chicago, Detroit, and Indianapolis. There were others too numerous to mention. The point is that half of the United States of America was up for sale and there were plenty of buyers. He needed someone to be his front man, someone to act on his behalf.

It was Monday afternoon and the meeting between Jimmy and Luke didn't go as planned.

Luke was quick, quicker than Jimmy had expected. Before he could react, Jimmy had two gaping holes in his chest and he was fading fast, and then he was gone.

Going through Jimmy's backpack, Luke only found a few pictures of some gold-embossed paper, nothing of any value.

He made a call. "Ms. Conley? The guy had nothing, he knew nothing and now he is nothing."

She closed her cell and frowned.

Monday night a visitor quietly disengaged the alarm system and slipped into the First National Bank through the back door. The figure, dressed in black, made its way to Jimmy's workspace and ransacked his desk; opened every file, every drawer. His computer was removed and loaded into a box and then the figure was gone. His apartment was next. After the shadowy figure finished rifling through, it disappeared—vanished without a trace with nothing, absolutely nothing!

Time was running out.

There was only one other person who could have stolen that document and he was late for work, thought Ms. Conley. It was Tuesday morning and her private line rang. There was only one person who would be calling and she knew who it was. As well connected as Pastor T.J. was, little passed his notice. The meeting with Ms. Conley, John, the former and current mayors, fire chief and sheriff was uncomfortable. Pastor T.J. made his point, and now they were highly motivated. Their lives depended on it. And with their newfound motivation, no stone was left unturned.

Ms. C. dialed Luke's cell for the third time.

"Luke, I need the recording you made last Saturday night now! I'll pay you double what I first said I'd pay."

"Triple."

"Okay, but do you know where Chase is? He is late for work."

"No, but I can find him for a fee."

"Just find him! Fast," she said as she closed her phone and slammed it on the desk.

That afternoon, she and John had the recording of the phone conversation between Jimmy and Chase and were pouring over its details. *So Jimmy had something after all, that little creep; Luke said he didn't*, Ms. C. mused.

"Maybe Luke has it now," John volunteered.

"I don't think so, he's not that bright, and I can tell when he's lying."

"What do you think Jimmy was talking about when he told Chase to expect his birthday gift in the mail? Why couldn't he just bring it to work?" John asked.

"He and Jimmy were not on each other's Christmas card list. I think that Jimmy was speaking metaphorically. He sent him something. The question is: what and where?"

"That's two questions and two different answers, and Chase knows both of them," John pointed out.

CHAPTER 16

Tuesday at Ronnie's Restaurant

It was Tuesday evening, and Chase and Megan met outside the door of their usual rendezvous spot called Ronnie's. It was a quaint little coffee shop a few blocks off the square. They entered through the front door that opened on Pine Street. From their vantage point they had a clear line of sight of any uninvited guests. As they made their way to an empty booth they noticed that the dinner crowd had dissipated and coffee hour hadn't quite hit yet. Except for another young couple dressed in Halloween costumes, sitting in a nearby booth, they were alone and could talk freely. Chase nodded in the usual manner to the young man, and he nodded rather absently back.

Megan had feelings for Chase, strong feelings. She cared for him and wanted to see him trust Christ.

"Despite our differences on religious issues," Megan said as she stirred her coffee, I would like to share my testimony with you, Chase."

"Okay M, I'm listening," Chase said reluctantly.

"It was hard for me to live my faith in a home like mine," she began. "My father took a rather open view when I made the decision to trust Christ. Back then he took the 'I'm okay, you're okay' position, that *all* religions lead to the same place and who's to say if anyone's view is better or worse than the others."

"That's kind of what your dad was preaching the other night. Don't you agree with him?"

"Actually no," Megan said softly. "I don't agree with him. All religions are not the same, and all roads don't lead to heaven. The Bible says:

> "Enter ye in at the strait gate: for wide is the gate, and broad is the way, that leadeth to destruction, and many there be which go in thereat."
>
> Matthew 7:13 (KJV)

"You see, Chase," Megan spoke earnestly, "there is only one way to get into heaven, and that is by trusting Christ as your Savior."

As Megan spoke, the conversation between the other couple ceased and it seemed that they were listening intently. From time to time Megan actually caught a glimpse of recognition from the young lady, and she thought, *She certainly is beautiful, I've never seen her around here before; I wonder who she is.*

90

Chase, feeling the pressure, changed the subject and asked, "What about your mom?"

"Mom was different. You see, I was raised in private schools with strict Muslim teachers. And yes, the lady teachers enjoyed the fruits of America's labors to set the Muslim people free; I heard their teachings, memorized large portions of the Qu'ran, and frankly agreed with a lot of their thinking. When the missionary to the Muslim people came to my school to give a counterview in my debate class, he said things that I had never heard before. He said that Jesus was the Son of God and that he and Allah were not one and the same. When he described the characteristic and demands of Allah (which I already knew) and compared them with the teachings of Jesus, there was no comparison. Then when he showed the class from the Bible that Jesus came to earth to die for other people's sins, frankly that shocked me. Allah would never have done that. Nor would any other deity. To top it off, he showed us from the Bible that Jesus' death, burial, and resurrection were all part of a master plan, prophesied centuries before it happened. I was hooked! I had to learn more. So over the next couple of weeks I met secretly with the missionary and then one day it happened."

"What happened?" Chase had been listening with half his brain. But when she said 'it happened,' Chase's interest piqued. The only thing that happened in his experience was some gibberish.

"I put my trust in the Lord Jesus Christ, that's what happened," she said with a smile.

"It was that simple? No tongues, no water, no laying on of hands?" Chase asked.

"No silly, I just put my faith in Jesus to forgive my sins and take me to heaven."

"How do you know that it's real, you're not in heaven yet?"

"God gave me the confidence through His Word. The Bible says:

> "That whosoever believeth in him should not perish, but have eternal life. For God so loved the world, that he gave his only begotten Son, that whosoever believeth in him should not perish, but have everlasting life."
>
> John 3:15–16 (KJV)

"It goes on to say,

> He that believeth on him is not condemned: but he that believeth not is condemned already, because he hath not believed in the name of the only begotten Son of God."
>
> John 3:18 (KJV)

By now she had her Bible open and was pointing with her finger to 1 John 5:10 and read:

> "He that believeth on the Son of God hath the witness in himself: he that believeth not God hath made him a liar; because he believeth not the record that God gave of his Son. These things have I written unto you that believe on the name of the

Son of God; that ye may know that ye have eternal life, and that ye may believe on the name of the Son of God."

1 John 5:10, 13 (KJV)

It wasn't the sweetness of Megan's voice or her earnestness that moved Chase to open his heart. It was the culmination of years of prayers; his dad and mom's prayers. They were finally answered. The Holy Spirit moved upon his heart and brought him to pray a simple prayer of faith and place his trust in Christ alone.

Chase experienced God's peace for the first time in his life now that salvation had become a reality.

Chase had the answer!

"What did your mom say when you told her that you became a Christian?"

"Well, actually I didn't use the word Christian. To a Muslim, a Christian is an infidel, an invader, and the enemy. In most countries Christians and Catholics are one and the same, and Muslims and Catholics have been at war with each other for centuries."

"Is your mom a Muslim?"

"No, but she would have reacted even worse if I had used that word."

"What did you tell her?"

"I told her the plain truth, that I trusted Christ to forgive my sins."

"What did she say to that?"

"She put a voodoo curse on me!" she smiled and said.

"A voodoo curse! Did it work?"

"Yep! I turned into a pumpkin!" Megan said with a chuckle.

"Seriously!"

"No, silly, it didn't work. 'Greater is He that is in me, than he that is in the world' 1 John 4:4 (KJV)."

As Megan continued to show Chase some additional verses to strengthen his faith, she inadvertently pointed to the wrong verse. Actually, there never was a wrong verse, because the Lord providentially guided her finger to 1 John 4:1.

> "Beloved, believe not every spirit, but try the spirits whether they are of God: because many false prophets are gone out into the world."
>
> 1 John 4:1 (KJV)

He interrupted Megan in mid-verse and asked, "What does that verse mean?"

She read the verse again out loud.

> "Beloved, believe not every spirit, but try the spirits whether they are of God: because many false prophets are gone out into the world."
>
> I John 4:1 (KJV)

"Well," she said thoughtfully, "John is saying the day will come when there will be a lot of confusion over the truth of the gospel. And that we must be discerning."

"What does 'try the spirits' mean?"

She nervously rubbed the back of her neck. "It means to investigate, to examine, to see if what these false teachers are saying is true. There are other verses that go along with that."

Megan opened her Bible to 2 Corinthians and read:

> "For such (are) false apostles, deceitful workers, transforming themselves into the apostles of Christ. And no marvel: for Satan himself is transformed into an angel of light. Therefore (it is) no great thing if his ministers also be as the ministers of righteousness; whose end shall be according to their works."
>
> 2 Corinthians 11:13–15 (KJV)

"Are you telling me that Satan can actually appear as a minister?" Chase said as he watched the lights come on in her mind.

Tears began to form in her eyes. "Do you think that my dad is the devil?"

"No, I don't think so M, but I'm not in the position to say; I do think that we have a problem." And with that Chase unpacked the story as he learned it. The story of the fraudulent loan applications, the story of the Middle Eastern bank accounts, the story of her father's ties to a radical Muslim cleric. He told her what he knew of The Order and the Document.

Chase couldn't help but notice how intently the good-looking young man in the other booth had been listening.

"There's just one more thing, Megan, I haven't seen Jimmy in a few days and frankly I'm worried about him. The last time we talked he said that he was sending me my birthday gift. Well, my birthday is not for another six months. But I did get a package from him labeled, 'Open if you don't see me by Tuesday.'"

Chase looked at the package, "Well, it's Tuesday. I haven't opened it yet, you want to open it now?"

"Let's do it," Megan said enthusiastically. Nervously he dug it out of his backpack. It was a small padded pouch-type envelope. He tore it open and out fell a key.

"What is it?" Megan asked curious to know.

"It's a key to a safe deposit box."

"What's a safe deposit box?" Megan asked naively.

"It's a safe in a bank where people put their valuables."

With heightened interest Megan asked, "What bank is the safe deposit box located in?"

"My bank. Ms. C.'s bank!

CHAPTER 17

Wednesday—First National
Bank of Beaumont

They waited outside the bank in Megan's SUV for John to show up. He didn't show. But Ms. C. did get an interesting phone call, however, and they watched her as she rushed out of the bank, leaving a skeleton crew to run the bank till closing.

"C'mon, M, let's go before I lose my nerve."

"How can we get into the safe deposit box vault and get the box open. Doesn't it take two keys?" Megan asked inquisitively.

"Yes, but I happen to be the CLO, and I can get the other key," Chase said rather confidently.

"I feel like a bank robber or something."

"Yeah, a regular Butch Cassidy and the Sundance Kid."

"Hey Chase," the receptionist said upon seeing him enter the bank, "Ms. C.'s been worried sick over you, where have you been?"

"I ... uh ... we were out looking for Jimmy, has he ever showed up?"

"Nope, but his desk and file cabinets have been torn all to pieces. Looks like someone was looking for something without asking for his permission."

"How did they get in, was there a break-in?"

"That's what the police are trying to find out, no alarms went off, yet someone clearly got in here and ransacked his office," the receptionist said.

"Did they attack my office?" Chase asked as he headed in that direction.

"As cluttered as your work space is, the thieves would still be in here trying to find the door."

"Don't get funny, this is serious."

"Well, all I know is that if you don't show up for work tomorrow you're going to get fired."

"Well, in that case, if I don't show up tomorrow, I'll quit!" he said with a smile.

Then Chase quickly retrieved the counter key to the safe deposit box and he and Megan entered the vault.

"This is scary," she said.

"Don't worry, M, we'll be out of here in a minute."

Chase used the two keys to unlock the drawer, and withdrew it from its shelf. He placed the long drawer on the table in the center of the room and carefully lifted up the lid. Chase pulled a rather large envelope from the drawer and replaced the lid and pushed the drawer back into its slot and closed the door. Then he turned his attention on the envelope.

"Let's not spend anymore time in here than we have to, M. Let's go some place safe to open this envelope and check out what's in it."

"I'll be glad to," and with that Megan turned and quickly left the vault. Chase was close on her heels. They made it safely to her SUV without any prying eyes noticing them. Megan started the SUV and pulled out into traffic.

"Where to? The usual coffee shop?" asked Megan.

"No, not this time, it's too risky. I need a place to hide out, where I can check this thing out. Do you have any ideas?"

"Yeah, Daddy has a chalet up off of Pine Ridge. No one will ever suspect you up there. I'm forever taking guests there for over night get-a-ways."

"Is anybody there now?"

"Nope, not till Friday."

"After Friday, one way or another I won't be needing it."

Megan headed out of town. When she got to Pine Ridge she turned and started up the incline. It took nearly an hour to get there, and in the meantime Chase opened the envelope and began reading the document. "M, I can't believe what I'm holding. If this thing is real, we are the rightful owners of half of the United States of America."

Megan nearly swerved off of the road as she tried to get a look at the document Chase was holding.

"Does this chalet have Internet capabilities?"

"If you thought my house was something, you ain't seen nothin' yet."

They pulled up as the sun gently faded from view. The shadows gave the chalet a rather ghostly appearance. The few lights that burned within the structure indicated that indeed it was unoccupied. The air was cool and refreshing. The sounds of evening already were starting to awaken.

"This place is magnificent. It must have taken a fortune to buy."

"It's been here for a number of years. Daddy bought it from a rich oil business man from Saudi Arabia."

"You don't say. I wonder if there is a connection with him and some of the money funding The Order?" Chase said thoughtfully. Megan had a concerned look on her face as she took out her key, unlocked the door, and let them in.

"Stand there for a minute while I disengage the alarm system."

After a moment she returned and smiled. "Well, home away from sweet home." Megan wasn't very enthusiastic as she pointed out some of the rooms in the sprawling get-a-way. Her mind was on other things. Questions were beginning to form in her mind. Things that she took for granted now came into question. *Who were these people? What did they want? Who is my dad?*

As Megan made her way back to the front door, she thought of one more thing to tell Chase.

"Chase, I'm a bit nervous to tell you this, and you may not even need to know, but in order to get to the third floor of my house where the bedrooms are, you need to know the security code…"

Chase wasn't quite sure of the ramifications of having such information. Surely this wasn't what he thought it was. "Megan, I'm not sure where you are going with this, but I'm not interested in our relationship going beyond being good friends." He still had Susan on the brain, and hadn't figured out how to tell Megan about her. Some things are best left unsaid.

"Whatever are you talking about? I'm about to tell you a sworn secret and you're thinking about what?"

Chase gulped and dropped his head in humiliation. "Oops!"

"You had better say 'oops!' I'm saving myself for marriage and wouldn't think of having a cheap fling with you or anybody else for that matter."

"Okay, okay, I said I'm sorry. I totally misread you."

"Whatever. What I was about to tell you before I was so rudely interrupted was the security code which takes you not only to the residential floor, but also to the conference room, which I might add is where the big shindig is supposed to happen this Friday. The code is my birthday: August twenty-first, 1989, so the code is two-one-zero-eight-one-nine-eight-nine."

"If your birthday is August twenty-first, 1989, shouldn't it be zero-eight-two-one-one-nine-eight-nine?"

"Nope, that's the American way of stating a birth date; the European way is as I said, two-one-zero-eight-one-nine-eight-nine. 'This tape recording will self destruct in five seconds.'"

"Oh! Okay I get it, and I just need to walk in there and hand over this very important document."

"Yeah, well, you figure it out and text me and I'll come get you. In the meantime I need to be getting back to the house before anyone suspects anything." And with that she turned abruptly and without so much as a good-bye, left.

Chase had the distinct feeling that he had hurt Megan's feelings. It hurt him to think that he could have been such a blockhead. It was bad enough that he was a wanted man by half the warlords in the world. Now he had women troubles, too.

He wasn't sure which was worse.

CHAPTER 18

Robber's Roost

Glenn Tibbits had not been idle. He and his friend John were on the look out for Chase in John's new BMW. Even if Glenn knew the whereabouts of Chase, he was not about to tell John. There were just too many unanswered questions for him to trust John with that sensitive information. What they needed to do was to go to Stan Berkowitz and blow the lid off this whole thing. Once it hit the paper there would be no place to hide. That was Chase's instructions.

"Aren't we going the long way around to get to the *Observer,* my friend?" Glenn said.

"I have a couple of stops to make before we get there."

"I sure hope none of them include the bank,"

"Now, what did ya mean by that? Just because we're members of the same bachelor's club doesn't mean that I have to stay one."

"Just kidding, don't get so testy."

The terrain got rougher as they made their way out to the area known as Robbers Roost.

"Hey, I remember this place. I used to come out here to hunt quail. What business do we have coming out here?"

"I got a call from Ms. C. earlier, and she asked me to check out Robbers Roost to see if Chase's car is there. Maybe if we see it or its tracks it will lead us to him."

"I see," Glenn said rather dubiously. What Glenn didn't see was the dark blue sedan with a dented front fender following them.

The location was not unfamiliar to Luke. He had been there before. It was his favorite place to ply his special ability. When John and Glenn got out of John's BMW, Luke seemed to appear out of nowhere. The meeting was brief, the discussion curt, his action swift, and the results...final.

John fell to the ground with a sickening thud, his life's blood flowing out of the hole in the back of his head. To Glenn this was all a dream, a nightmare! In his entire life, he had never seen someone die like that. Oh, he had seen people die, but never like that. His wife died in his arms with the name of Jesus on her lips.

This was different.

There's nothing like looking at a loaded gun to clear one's memory.

Glenn wanted to run but his feet were like lead. He just stood there waiting for his turn to die. He was ready. But death never came.

Luke stood there with a wolfish grin. "Okay, ole man, where's Chase and where's the document?"

Glenn had no clue where either Chase or the document was.

"Even if I knew that information, which I don't, I wouldn't tell you. I can see what you would do with me and Chase if you had it."

"I heard Jimmy say that he was sending Chase a birthday gift. Well, I happen to know that Chase's birthday ain't for another six months 'cause I crashed his birthday party last year and got kicked out and spent the night in the poky. So, where is this gift?"

"I don't know," Glenn said earnestly. He had to stall for time.

"Okay, ole man, let's take a ride. You drive and no funny business."

"Where are we going?"

"Just be quiet and drive, I'll tell you where once we get back to the main road," Luke said with malice in his voice.

Once they got to the main road, Luke told Glenn to turn right and head back to town as fast as possible.

Glenn finally got a chance to take a joy ride in a stolen BMW, but there was no joy in this ride.

As chance would have it, Glenn had a bad habit of running red lights. He seemed to always be late and that was the quickest way to make up time. Plus, he didn't see that well. At least that was what he told Sheriff Conyers every time he got pulled over. This time it worked in his favor. As they sped through yet another red light neither Glenn nor Luke saw the pick-up truck approaching from the passenger's side. The impact sent John's car careening across the intersection. When the vehicle stopped rolling, it sat on its passenger side, and Luke was missing. His remains were found in a drainage ditch a few yards away.

He had received his reward.

Glenn was pretty banged up, but survived, as did the driver of the pick-up truck. Before the ambulance and sheriff arrived, Glenn got out of the car and was found sitting in the back of the pick-up swapping fishing stories with its driver. Being taken to the hospital was not part of Glenn's plan. At least Chase's whereabouts would remain safe.

Or so he thought.

Friday—The City Jail

The sheriff had his own agenda and it didn't include a visit to the hospital either. He headed straight to the city jail.

"Now, Sheriff, you don't have to get all law-abiding just because some killer got his just desserts, do ya?"

"Somebody has gotta pay," the sheriff said ruefully.

"Now, where have I heard that before?"

"There's someone I think you should meet and the only place where it's safe is at the jail. My deputy will see to that."

As they approached the city jail, Glenn noticed an ambulance from the adjoining county was parked in one of the slots along with several federal cars marked ATF and FBI. There were also a number of heavily armed SWAT teams standing around one of the tactical vehicles smoking and talking quietly. As Glenn and the sheriff faced the men they saluted as they stood at attention.

"What's all this about?"

"Come inside and I'll explain the whole thing, but we'd better get a move on, things are heating up at the pastor's house." Glenn gave the sheriff a puzzled look and went in. Inside the jailhouse was a virtual boiler room of activity. What was usually a quiet "Andy of Mayberry" type of jail was now a command post for a major military operation. There was a bank of computers set up along the back wall, a communication center in the first of two jail cells, and a large map diagramming the layout of the pastor's house. There was a satellite feeding images of the grounds to several big screen TVs and the SWAT team commander monitoring the activities. In the middle of it all was Susan wearing bandages and being held up with a set of crutches. Though badly injured, she was standing up and giving vital information to her boss and other official-looking people. The press, with the exception of Stan Berkowitz, was being held at bay by two of Sheriff Conyers' deputies.

"Well, what happened to you, honey?"

"Honey! You know this woman?" the sheriff said rather incredulously.

"Yes, sir, she's my daughter."

"Your daughter? When did that happen?"

"Oh, about forty years ago, give or take," Glenn said not wanting to reveal his daughters true age. Glenn, looking concerned, turned back to Susan.

"What happened?"

"Someone tried to kill me. Fortunately Sheriff Conyers was in the area and happened to see the whole thing. He rescued me and called in the emergency. Mercy Hospital sent a rescue squad and a helicopter. They took me to the hospital."

"I hadn't heard anything about this, when did this happen?"

"The Friday night after Chase and I discovered all the fraudulent stuff about the pastor and most of the church members. I've been hiding out at the county hospital over in Bradenton."

"And you brought all of your friends to this party?"

"Once I got in touch with our … my boss, and he contacted his boss, it all hit the fan. We just need to find Chase before the bad guys do. Do you know where he is?"

"That's what everybody's been asking me and I haven't the slightest clue."

Just then the FBI field commander stepped up and interrupted the conversation. "Sir, we have Intel that there is something going on up there at the pastor's residence. We need to move out. If they have captured Chase his life may be in grave danger."

Glenn said a silent prayer.

The road leading to Pastor T. J.'s palatial home was long and winding. By the time everyone was assigned a vehicle, they had lost fifteen minutes. It took the caravan thirty minutes to drive the distance from downtown to the front gate of the pastor's sprawling estate. To look at the caravan leaving town, one would have thought it was either a state funeral or a Fourth of July parade. Susan and Glenn rode in the patrol car driven by Sheriff Conyers.

He had heard Glenn say that Susan was his daughter, but he didn't even know he had a daughter, let alone that it might be Susan.

"So, Susan, fill me in about being Glenn's daughter."

"Well, Sheriff, actually, my name isn't Susan Bailes; it's Jennifer Ridly. Glenn is my step-dad; he married my mom after my dad was killed in the war. We both work for the FBI in the SI Unit, the Special Investigations Unit, and we've been following this cult called The Order for years."

Glenn chimed in. "I grew up in this town as a boy, this church is my home. My roots go deep here. When I heard that the cult called The Order was planning to move its headquarters here, I was the first to volunteer to come back and reestablish my roots."

"Re-establish your roots, where did you go?"

"Well, during the war, I was in intelligence. I did a lot of in-field surveillance and some espionage. After the war I married Jennifer's mother, and moved to Virginia to be closer to her family.

Jennifer's mother died of breast cancer a few years later.

"So that's why she has a different name," the sheriff mused.

"The FBI drafted me, and for years I was a field agent when they developed the SI Unit and I was inducted into it," Glenn continued.

"She certainly doesn't resemble you in the least, thank the Lord," Sheriff Conyers quipped.

"She's a spitting image of her mother."

Glenn continued unpacking the story. "They knew that 'The Dean' was operating in the area recruiting talented people into the organization. They also knew that he had a bad habit of buying handcrafted jewelry so I was set up as a jeweler. Soon, he and I had a thriving business relationship together. He spent a lot of his or his church's money in my shop. So when I learned that the Order was moving to this town, I came here as a retired jeweler—that was my cover."

"Well, what is this Order anyway?" the sheriff asked incredulously.

Glenn cleared his throat and continued the story. "It's a long story, but the organization has its roots as far back as the time of the Crusaders, only they were not the Crusaders. The Crusaders or the Crusades were a series of religiously sanctioned military campaigns waged by much of western Christian Europe. They were commissioned by the Catholic Church to retake the Holy Land and claim it for the Church. It seemed that the pope and all sequential popes believe in the Replacement Theology."

"Now, what the heck is the Replacement Theology?" the Sheriff asked.

"That's the belief that the Catholic Church has replaced Israel in God's divine plan and that all the promises given to Abraham and the Patriarchs now belong to the Church."

"What does that have to do with The Order?"

"It seems that when the Crusaders got to the Holy Land it was inhabited by the Turks, an Arab brand of Muslims living there. The Holy Land was fought over for more than 200 years and changed hands about as many times. The crusades were also conducted against the Slavs,

Balts, Jews, Russian and Greek Orthodox Christians, Hussites, and Prussians to name just a few. From these countries formed a consortium of wealthy landholders; among them were some kings, princes of the besieged lands. They formed an underground network, which plotted to kill whichever pope was in power at the time.

The sheriff was intrigued by this time. "Did they succeed?"

"Sometimes and sometimes not, but they paid a terrible price. Over the centuries the network got better organized until it started calling itself The Order. And they are committed to the cause of overthrowing anything that is Christian/Catholic, free enterprise, and pro-Jewish. It has been instrumental in most, if not all, of the wars in Europe," said Glenn.

"And most of the revolutions as well," Susan chimed in.

"So, how did they get here and what does it have to do with America?" the sheriff asked probingly.

"As I said," Susan continued, "they were involved in most of the revolutions, including the American Revolution, and I might add the American Civil War."

"Yes!" Glenn said, "The Order has been infiltrating this country since its founding."

"Well, when was the last time they did anything here in the U.S.?" Conyers asked.

"The last major move they made on this country was in the years leading up to and throughout the Great Depression," Glenn said.

"The Great Depression! That wasn't all that long ago. How'd they do that?" asked the sheriff.

"You remember that before October twenty-ninth, 1929, better known as Black Tuesday, America was shackled with massive debt. Banks were loaning money at a rate of nine to one. A borrower could borrow nine dollars with only one dollar of collateral. When the crash that followed Black Tuesday happened, the Federal Reserve Banks couldn't cover the outstanding debt, and like a house of cards, banks failed, businesses failed, people lost their homes and were living on the street. Some economists say that it took World War II to finally get us out." Glenn knew his history. "Many believe that The Order had so infiltrated the government and the banking industry that they actually caused the Great Depression, hoping to capitalize on our misfortune. They nearly succeeded. How we defeated them at the last minute will forever be a top classified secret. I wasn't involved in it, but I knew people, very important people who were."

Susan picked up the story. "Really the last major action that The Order allegedly took against America in the last fifty years is thought to have been the assassination of President Kennedy. You recall that he was a Catholic. And since they have a history of assassination against popes, it is not too much of a stretch to think that they were behind that as well." Susan paused. "Although we don't actually have hard proof."

"What gave you the idea that this Order thing was going to do something now-a-days?" the sheriff wondered out loud.

"The same scenario which preceded the Great Depression is in place across most of the U.S., and because the President is loath to go to war, we think we are vulnerable to The Order. We know that we have been infiltrated, we just don't know who is on whose side. That's why I couldn't trust John. We had spent so much time fishing together, I actually thought that he was one of them," Glenn said sadly.

"How did you learn that The Order was coming here?" the sheriff asked.

"The Dean accidentally let it slip. He paid dearly for his mistake. You see, he was the one who The Order was planning on installing as the pastor of the First Church. But because of his slip of the tongue, he was forced into retirement, and Pastor T.J. replaced him. Not knowing that I was an FBI informant when I moved back to Beaumont, he called me and recommended T.J. for the pastorate. I was behind the whole thing in getting him in position.

"So, how did Su ... Jennifer get involved."

"You can call me Susan," she said. "They drafted me after I finished my tour of duty in Iraq. You see, when I finished college I enlisted in the Air Force and was trained to fly those drones. In a way I was in surveillance as well, only my drones were armed with missiles. I was responsible for cleaning out a lot of the 'close-in' targets in Kandahar and Mosul before the ground forces moved in. Because of my background the FBI's SI unit was quite interested in training me to do surveillance for them. I've been with the unit for about a year now. When Dad volunteered for this mission, he drafted me to be his backup plan."

Glenn continued to unpack the story: "So when I was in place, I was looking for a way to infiltrate The Order. Then Chase stepped into the picture. He was the perfect alibi to get Susan into the bank and look at the records."

"Do you mean to say that Chase is in on this thing, too?"

"No, not at all," Susan said. "He happened to be in the right place at the right time."

"Well, because of my position in the church and in the city, I used my pull to get Chase the job rather than Jimmy. Chase actually made a pretty good CLO. If he ever needs a part-time job I'm certain the bank will hire him back."

"He could pass as a bank examiner as well," Susan quipped.

"So could you, my dear, so could you."

"Now, Dad! I was inserted to look into the backgrounds of the people moving into town. We had heard about a very important document, but we didn't know what it was. I was supposed to keep my eyes open for it and find out what it was and report back to Glenn…uh…Dad, who then would pass the Intel on. The problem is that Jimmy got to it first and it got him killed."

"It nearly got me killed as well. I really feel bad about John."

"What about John? I thought he was one of them."

"That's what everyone was supposed to think. He was a plant, too. The FBI recruited him after he had joined The Order. He was deep throat. No one but a very few even knew that he was one of us. His job was to keep an eye open for the document and steal it if he found it. His mistake happened when he didn't recognize it or didn't see it when it was lying right there on Ms. C.'s desk. Then Jimmy got it and that complicated matters tremendously. I only learned that John was one of us, moments before he was shot. He turned to me and gave me a signal that only members of the SI unit knew. We were to use it if we felt we were in grave danger. He died for a good cause," Glenn said sadly.

Susan turned to her father and spoke softly, "I hope he gets the honors he deserves."

"He'll get a full military burial in the Arlington National Cemetery."

"So, you and Glenn were in cahoots together right under my very impressive nose, and I didn't even know it."

"That's our job," Glenn said, "to keep a low profile."

"Well it nearly got you killed, too, Susan. Fortunately I was doing my own surveillance. Do you think the FBI could use a guy like me?"

"I think they have an age limit now-days," Glenn said with a smile as they arrived at the pastor's house.

Chapter 19

Friday—several hours earlier…

Chase sat at the kitchen table drinking coffee from a mug and studying the document. Actually, it was more than a single sheet of paper. It was many sheets of paper, all saying basically the same thing. Each page was a legal description of a large landmass, using points and degrees to describe landmarks and boundary lines. Much of it dated back to the time of Lewis and Clark, two rugged men who forged the western passage. The Lewis and Clark Expedition (1804–1806) was the first overland expedition undertaken by the United States to the Pacific Coast and back. Their journey took them across what is now Kansas, Missouri, Nebraska, Iowa, North Dakota, and Oregon.

At the bottom of each page was a paragraph full of language spelling out the transfer of ownership from the former owner of the United States of America to The Order. All that was necessary for this transaction to be official was two signatures and their witnesses. The ramifications of this transfer of ownership were overwhelming to Chase. It meant that nearly half of the United States of America would no longer be under its jurisdiction. States such as: North and South Dakota, Nebraska, Kansas, Oklahoma, Texas, New Mexico, Colorado. Wyoming, Montana, Idaho, Utah, Arizona, Nevada, California, Oregon, and Washington all would fall under this decree if this document were ratified.

If this transaction takes place, millions of Americans living in those states will wake up no longer Americans. And the odds were that The Order would not be satisfied with having the mid and western states. Chase could see in his mind's eye that something even bigger was afoot.

They had to be stopped! But how? Chase thought to himself. *Should I destroy the document? Would that stop The Order?*

At that moment, Chase's life hung by a thread and time was running out.

He picked up his cell phone and began to text Megan, hoping that she was free to get away and pick him up. He wasn't sure what he was going to do, but he couldn't just sit idly by. He had to do something.

Megan made her way to the chalet without being missed by her parents, as guests and dignitaries began to arrive.

"M, I'm glad to see you. This thing is big, really big, and if we don't stop it we are all going to wake up tomorrow as citizens of a foreign and hostile nation."

"What will we do, what can we do?"

"I'm not sure what, M, but I'm not staying here. Let's talk about it as we drive."

"Where? Where are we going?" Her concern was written all over her pretty face, and it grieved Chase to see her in such consternation.

"I dunno, the one place we should be avoiding is the one place we need to get to, and it's the one place where we will be in the most danger ... the conference center."

As they drove, Chase began mapping out a plan of action. "It isn't much, but maybe, *just maybe*, with God's help we can stop this thing dead in its tracks."

Suddenly Megan put on her brakes and screeched to a stop. There they sat, right in front of a little church called the House of Prayer Chapel.

"You know, you said with God's help we can stop this thing, yet we haven't asked one time for God's help. Maybe we should."

Chase looked over at the chapel and then back to Megan. "No maybe about it, let's go inside and start asking."

She parked the SUV near the front of the chapel and found the door unlocked, and they entered in. The place was quiet, very quiet, almost sound proof. The noise of the outside traffic was imperceptible. On the walls of the chapel were Scripture verses. They began walking around the room reading the verses.

"If my people, who are called by my name, will humble themselves and pray and seek my face and turn from their wicked ways, then will I hear from heaven and will forgive their sin and will heal their land."

2 Chronicles 7:14 (KJV)

"And (Jesus) said unto them, It is written, My house shall be called the house of prayer; but ye have made it a den of thieves. And all things, whatsoever ye shall ask in prayer, believing, ye shall receive."

Matthew 21:13 (KJV)

"Rejoicing in hope; patient in tribulation; continuing instant in prayer."

Romans 12:12 (KJV)

"Now I beseech you, brethren, for the Lord Jesus Christ's sake, and for the love of the Spirit, that ye strive together with me in your prayers to God for me."

Romans 15:30 (KJV)

"Praying always with all prayer and supplication in the Spirit, and watching thereunto with all perseverance and supplication for all saints."

Ephesians 6:18 (KJV)

"Be careful for nothing; but in every thing by prayer and supplication with thanksgiving let your requests be made known unto God."

Philippians 4:6 (KJV)

"I exhort therefore, that, first of all, supplications, prayers, intercessions, [and] giving of thanks, be made for all men; for kings, and [for] all that are in authority; that we may lead a quiet and peaceable life in all godliness and honesty."

1 Timothy 2:1–2 (KJV)

"For we wrestle not against flesh and blood, but against principalities, against powers, against the rulers of the darkness of this world, against spiritual wickedness in high places."

Ephesians 6:12 (KJV)

"Submit yourselves therefore to God. Resist the devil, and he will flee from you. Draw nigh to God and He will draw nigh to thee."

James 4:7–8 (KJV)

Chase stood in front of this verse, which was mounted on the wall and read it out loud. "What does this verse mean, 'Resist the devil and he will flee from you,' James 4:7. Do you mean to say that the devil can be defeated?"

Megan came over and stood looking at the plaque and read it again. "Actually, the devil has already been defeated when Jesus rose from the dead. Satan is a defeated foe, and we are on the winning side."

"That's great news to hear, but if we don't act fast he's about to score a pretty substantial comeback."

"Satan's ultimate doom is spelled out in the book of the Revelation. I've been studying it on my own and there is a verse you need to read."

Megan proceeded to root through her handbag. She pulled out her New Testament and opened it, and read, "And they overcame him by the blood of the Lamb, and by the word of their testimony" Revelation 12:11 (KJV).

"That's it, M, we need to claim the blood of Jesus and our testimony that he is our Lord and Savior when we go into that conference center."

"Then we had better be prayed up before we go; look at the next plaque," she pointed to the plaque that read: "The effectual fervent prayer of a righteous man availeth much." James 5:16 (KJV)

Chase and Megan spent the next several hours claiming the promises in prayer. When they finished they knew what they had to do.

Upon arriving at the front gate, Sheriff Conyers, the field commander of the FBI, the deputy commander of the ATF, and the SWAT teams stopped. Armed guards holding the gated area met them. The gate area was sandbagged, and there were machine gun pits on either side of it. Some of the SWAT teams were quickly deployed around to the back gate located on the west side of the property while others took up positions behind the APCs prepared to fire their weapons if and when the command was given. Once everyone was in place the commander, armed with a no-knock warrant, boldly approached the gate and demanded that they open the gate and allow them to enter the property.

The captain of the guard was not impressed with the show of force. He spoke defiantly. "This is private property and the sovereign nation of The United States of the West. You have no justification here!"

"What do you mean the sovereign nation of The United States of the West? I know nothing of states seceding from the Union," the field commander retorted.

"Within the hour you and your infidel nation will, and then you will learn the wrath of Allah." Then he shouted: "Allah al Akbar! God is great."

Someone within the compound fired his weapon and a firefight ensued. When the smoke cleared all of the enemy combatants were either dead or dying. The field commander proceeded to have one of his men blow the lock on the gate.

The resistance at the south gate was light and quickly dispatched. With that, the caravan proceeded up the long driveway with their sirens blaring.

Chapter 20

Friday Afternoon–The
Conference of The Order

Three hours earlier Pastor T.J.'s house and conference center was a bevy of activity. Dignitaries and their entourages were arriving by the minute. The waiting area was a-buzz with conversations, many of which were being conducted in the languages of the countries being represented. There were Sheiks, and Swamis, Muslims from both sides of the isle, Buddhist Monks from the Himalayas, Indian clerics, Native America witch doctors, and Spiritists, as well as Hindu Priests and members of the Baha'i and Shinto religions, all dressed in their full regalia. It was like a bar scene from the movie *Star Wars*.

In the middle of the cacophony stood Pastor T.J. encouraging the revelry by ordering more wine and champagne for everyone. The waiters and waitresses were kept busy bringing out trays of hors d'oeuvres, such as lobster scampi puff, artichoke and spinach filo tartel, and edamame dumplings. There was an endless supply of the world's finest wines and champagne served in fine crystal stemware. He had spared no expense, nothing but the best. This was a night to be remembered, and he was the center of it.

More dignitaries began arriving, political dignitaries. There were heads of state or their representatives from China, the Middle East, South America, France, Germany, Great Britain, Russia, Libya, Yemen, and parts of Africa. Nearly the whole United Nations was represented at the gathering. Two nations were conspicuously absent: the United States of America and Israel.

They were not represented. They were not invited. They were not welcome.

"M, how are we going to get inside the fence without being detected?" Chase said as they approached her father's property.

"There's a service road on the south side of our property, the gate is just a cattle gate and seldom guarded. But, what with all the dignitaries, I'm sure there will be armed guards patrolling the whole grounds. Why don't you climb to the back and throw that canvas tarp over you, and if I'm stopped I'll try to talk my way out of being searched."

Chase climbed back and covered up as the SUV crossed over the cattle gate. Megan wasn't a hundred yards within the compound before an armored patrol vehicle approached her. The men inside were not the usual men who guarded the property. They were foreign Middle Eastern men, heavily armed and not very friendly.

"What are you doing coming on this property? This is private property, and you are intruding! I demand that you identify yourself!" the self appointed leader said with a thick accent.

Megan recognized his country of origin and spoke to him in his native language. "I am Megan Richards, daughter of Pastor T.J. Richards, and I demand that you identify yourselves. Who are you and why are you pointing that weapon at an unarmed woman?"

The shock and amazement of the face of the guard made it all worthwhile. He took a step back and looked at the other men. He turned and spoke to them; obviously he was conferring with them as to what to do. Finally he returned to the side of the SUV and spoke apologetically.

"Please do forgive my insolence, my most honorable lady. You may proceed, and Al hamdu lillah, may Allah smile on your venture."

Chase nearly split a seam trying to control his laughter as he heard the guard say "my most honorable lady." But he held it together and if he lived through the day, would have a LOL, a laugh out loud moment.

Megan made it to the boat garage door and hit the remote. Quietly the door opened and she guided the SUV into the empty bay. Obviously they were using the boat to patrol the huge man-made lake on the back of the property. The garage door returned to its former position without raising any alarms.

They were in!

They got out of her SUV and made their way through the service entrance to where the deliveries are made.

"Now that we're in, how are we supposed to get to the third floor without getting shot?" Chase whispered as they peeped through the crack in the kitchen door.

Megan looked around and said, "Quick, put on one of these waiter's jackets and follow me."

With that she stepped into the kitchen, which was a cauldron of activity and found a tray of hors d'oeuvres and handed it to Chase.

"Here, carry this tray and follow me."

She headed straight to the service elevator, which led to the third floor.

"This elevator is used only by the servants...I mean, kitchen staff, and won't be as heavily guarded as the main elevator."

She hit the third floor button and the doors closed. The elevator quickly rose to the third floor and the doors opened in a restricted area. The only guard was standing outside the door watching the servers coming and going. It wasn't unusual for him to help himself to one of the glasses of wine, champagne, or some of the hors d'oeuvres being carried to the guests. His eyes were already blood-shot and he looked a bit unstable on his feet.

"I don't think that they are expecting us to crash the party, and if we can get past the guard at the door, we've got a clear shot at getting into the main conference room. What you do then is up to you."

"I've got your Bible along with the document and this cigarette lighter I picked up as we were coming in, and I'm working on a plan now."

Megan nodded, smiled, squeezed his hand, and said, "I'll be praying for you the whole time and waiting for you in the back when the victory is won."

Chapter 21

*Friday Evening–The
Conference of The Order*

The guests and dignitaries soon were ushered into the conference room and took their seats.

"Let the meeting of The Order be officially called to order." And with that, Pastor T.J. Richards slammed down the gavel.

"Ladies, gentlemen, and esteemed guests, this day is marked by disappointment."

Pastor T.J. scanned the room as if to say, "I'm in command!"

"The document, which we have guarded at great cost to ourselves, which we have entrusted to Ms. Conley, our sister in the struggle, has been ... *misplaced*."

Pastor T.J. waited for the full effect to settle in.

The crowd gasped in horror!

He continued, "For years we have worked and planned and dreamed for this day, the Day of Consummation, only to have it ripped away from us."

He again paused, waiting for the murmuring to subside.

"Without that document we have no mandate, we have no power! We must use all the powers of our kinetic energy to draw us, to lead us, to guide us to that which was lost, to that which was stolen from us."

He again scanned the assembled luminaries as if looking for the perpetrator.

"We must also punish the evildoers."

The assembled crowd murmured their assent.

"What should be done with the one who has taken our beloved document?"

"Death to the infidel!"

"Death to the infidel!"

"Death to the infidel!"

The frenzied crowd began to chant.

"That sentence has already been carried out. What should be done to the ones who allowed this tragedy to occur in the first place?"

The assembly, thirsty for blood, cried out, "Death to the traitors, death to those who would bring death to us!"

He spoke again as if he were egging them on.

"Already one of the perpetrators has paid with his life, and now it is time for the other one." And with that Pastor T.J. stepped up behind the unsuspecting Ms. C. and slit her throat, to the horror and glee of the possessed audience. As if he were the high priest conducting an evil human sacrifice, Pastor T.J. spoke. His voice was thick with emotion as he addressed the hovering spirits within the conference hall.

"With this blood sacrifice I call upon the dark forces to lead us, to guide us, to reveal to us the one who has stolen our beloved document."

The lights of the room dimmed as the presence of the evil one moved within the minds of the congregates. The sound of murmuring began as those with familiar spirits slipped into trances while others chanted phrases over and over again. The room moaned as the volume increased to a fevered pitch.

Pastor T.J. lorded over the cacophony and smiled. He broke up the prayer meeting with a new set of radical statements designed to whip the assembled into an emotional frenzy.

"Too long have we been oppressed by the infidels and Jews. Too long have the dark forces inhabited our lands. Too long have we stood silently by and watched the enemy devour the fruit of our labors. *Too long* have we watched them steal our children and brainwash them with the poison of capitalism, of commercialism, and of Christianity. *Too long* have our streets been filled with the blood of our brothers, our sisters, our mothers, and our fathers. It is time we take back that which is rightfully ours, the land that was given to us by the Great Spirit. The lands of our brothers the Apaches, the Sioux, the Arapaho, and the Black Foot; lands that have been our ancestral home since the beginning of time. The spirits of our fathers cannot rest until all is made right. The Great Spirit within is stirring, is moving, and we must act."

He paused to collect his thoughts. He spoke as if he were a possessed man. He needed no notes; this was coming from deep within, from the very depths of the dark world.

"With this document we will have our mandate. We will form a coalition called the United States of the West, and declare war on the infidels to the East. Once we have achieved the inevitable victory, we will then drive the Jews into the sea!"

The frenzied crowd began chanting: "Death to the East, death to the West, death to those who would bring death to us."

As the chanting grew stronger, so too did the power of the evil one as he drank their anger as a witch's brew.

The door quietly swung open, and Megan, escorted by Chase, slipped into the conference room. Pastor T.J. had not noticed. In his rant, all eyes were riveted on him. No one could take their eyes off of him even if they wanted to. Even in a fit of rage his eloquence, his power of persuasion, was having its full effect. People heard what *he* wanted them to hear. They saw what *he* wanted them to see. This was not unlike a typical Saturday night or Sunday morning service. He could speak with such passion that if he wanted to, he could convince any audience that the sun revolves around the earth. His skill and mastery of the spirit language was mesmerizing. The audience was carried along wherever he led them. Years earlier, he had given himself over to the evil one to be his voice, his representative, his body! Now he was feeling his power!

Megan had heard it all before but she had never seen her father like this. His visage, the very look on his face had changed. His eyes once warm and tender now burned as hot embers. His voice, once inviting, was shrill and piercing. Only those who trusted Christ could resist him. Her faith made her strong and she prayed. "Resist the devil and he will flee from you, James 4:7," she claimed.

"Resist the devil and he will flee from you," James 4:7, kept echoing in Chase's mind as well. Since he was new to the faith, he had a much harder time focusing his attention on the task at hand. T.J.'s voice got into his head. Chase heard what he was saying in the room, but he heard another voice telling him to hand over the document, to give up on his quest for the truth. Then the peace of God that passes all understanding began to guard his mind. He heard the voice of God saying: "This is the way, walk ye in it," (Isaiah 30:21, KJV).

Chase claimed the promises and started walking! Suddenly the memory of an Old Testament story reverberated in Chase's mind. It was the story of David and Goliath. His mother had read that story to him countless times and it became one of his favorites. He spoke as he made his way to the podium with the document in hand, and Pastor T.J. retreated as a shadow in the light.

"Thou comest to me with a sword, and with a spear, and with a shield: but I come to thee in the

name of the LORD of hosts, the God of the armies
of Israel, whom thou hast defied."

1 Samuel 17:45 (KJV)

"Ladies and gentlemen of the Order, your expectation
has been dashed asunder, your hope is denied, and your
plans have been foiled. *You have failed!*" With that, Chase
held up the document and the cigarette lighter, and with
one smooth movement, he lit the document on fire and
held it up as if holding an Olympic torch. The flame lit
the room, and the spell was broken. As Chase spoke the
sound of sirens pierced the afternoon sky and the minds
of the audience. They were shocked to see their treasurer
bleeding to death on the floor and their esteemed leader
cowering in the corner.

Sheriff Conyers, flanked by Glenn, FBI, and ATF
agents rushed into the room with their weapons drawn.
The SWAT teams deployed themselves around the room,
thus, surrounding the guests.

It all became clear what Pastor T.J. had to do. The
doors that led to the third floor balcony were open. Below
it was the paved fountain area. The fall, though not far,
would be sufficient to kill most people, but that was not
Pastor T.J.'s plan.

He jumped!

His body was never recovered. Hours of searching the
premises proved fruitless. Pastor T.J. was gone.

Somewhere in southern California, a pulpit committee was being wowed by a smooth voice.

CHAPTER 22

The City Jail

Because many of the dignitaries and ambassadors had dip-lomatic immunity, most of them had to be released. Those who were found on Interpol's wanted list were detained and held in the city jail before they were transferred to the county seat and on into the federal judicial system.

Many of the membership of the Community First Church were arrested for falsifying loan documents and treason.

The following weeks were filled with evidence gather-ing, paperwork, interviews, debriefings, and more paper-work. Megan found it difficult to find Chase and even harder to talk to him. He was definitely up to his ears in the investigation.

Soon the first news release hit the papers. Not the *Beaumont Observer*, but the really big newspapers, and the television news outlets as well. Chase had beaten the talk show hosts by a mile. He was even being interviewed on all the big-named talk shows. His newfound notoriety even got him a book deal as well.

By now Glenn and Susan had returned to Washington, D.C. for the inevitable hearings, and then on to other assignments. Glenn and Susan never returned to Beaumont. Their cover had been compromised and so they were assigned to desk jobs, awaiting advancement within the SI Unit. Eventually, they both were promoted to very powerful and influential positions, ones that gave them access to sensitive information, information on a new and growing evil, an evil that concerned them very much. It also gave them the ability to monitor the activities of private citizens. One private citizen, who was of interest to Jennifer, AKA Susan Bailes, was a young investigative reporter by the name of Chase Newton, now with the *New York Times* and part of the Press Corps. She hoped very much to work with him again.

CHAPTER 23

The Courthouse

One day in between appointments and interviews, Chase got a chance to talk to Megan.

"Hey M, how have you been?"

"I've been a bit overwhelmed, what with my dad disappearing … literally, and with my mom fleeing the country. I've been at a loss for what to do next. I did find out that since Mom is a fugitive of the law and on nearly every country's most wanted list, that the government is seizing the house and all its property. Their bank accounts have been frozen, and I have to leave my home in just a few days." She started to cry.

It hurt Chase to see Megan this way. His mind was racing to think of something he could do.

"M, wait, I remember something I found when I was investigating your dad and mom's accounts. Let's go to my off … my old office and see if I can find it."

They made their way from the courthouse where the new investigation hub was housed to the bank across the street.

"Do you remember a lifetime ago nearly running over me as I was crossing this very street?" Chase asked trying to get Megan's mind off of her troubles.

"Yes. Yes, I do and as I said it was Dad driving."

"I distinctly remember a very pretty blond driving the SUV and waving a hand at me."

Sheepishly Megan looked at Chase. "Yes, it was me, but I wasn't actually trying to run over you. I was just trying to get your attention. I figured that would do it."

"Well, it certainly made an impression on me. As a matter of fact, that may have been the very thing that started off my investigation of The Order in the first place." They entered the bank and were quickly greeted by the receptionist and the new bank manager.

"Chase, Megan, it is so good to see you again. What can we do for you folks today?"

"When I was working here and doing background checks I discovered that Pastor T.J. had a number of off-shore bank accounts in Megan's name. Now the government is seizing all of the pastor's assets including the house, the property, everything. And Megan is going to be homeless in a few days. What about those off-shore accounts? Are they Megan's or are they going to be seized, too?"

"Well, let's go and look at them and see."

With that, the bank manager led them into her office and logged on to her computer.

"Let's start by bringing up those bank account numbers. Chase, do you have them?"

"Yes, they are here in my briefcase. I kept a copy of all my notes and findings in the event that I am called to Washington, D.C. again for yet another hearing."

He handed the bank manager a paper with four off-shore bank account numbers. She entered the numbers into the computer and in a moment let out a whistle. "It looks like you are a very wealthy young woman, Miss Megan. Those accounts are yours and the government can't get their hands on the money."

Megan looking rather surprised, said, "How much is in those accounts?"

"Let me see here," she said as she reached over and turned on her calculator. "The first account has $250,000 in it. The second has $750,500; the third is the big one, it has $1,000,000, and the fourth has $500,000. I'd say that you might be the newest and prettiest multi-millionaire that this bank has ever had."

Megan was overwhelmed with emotion. Chase leaned over, stroked her hair back from her face, and looked at her. "Looks like you'll be buying the next time we go to the coffee shop."

Afterword

Thank you for reading *Stranger in the Pulpit*. It is my sincere hope that you enjoyed the novel. It was my goal on the out-set to write a plausible story and make a few points about the state of the church in this post-modern era along the way.

You may have noticed the condition of The First Church. It was weak and carnal. They were easily impressed with outside appearances and they had no biblical foundation when it came to doctrine. Could this have happened today? It may not happen as I have described it, but it is happening at an alarming rate with New Age philosophy, and Post-Modern theology creeping into pulpits all over America.

Could our country be sold out right from under our noses? Probably not as I have proposed. But God did allow Israel to be sold into slavery to her enemies, and it's only by God's grace that it hasn't happened to us.

Thomas Jefferson said it best: "Eternal vigilance is the price of liberty." We must be vigilant and prayerful for our churches and nation in these last days.

> "If my people, who are called by my name, will humble themselves and pray and seek my face and turn from their wicked ways, then will I hear from heaven and will forgive their sin and will heal their land."
>
> 2 Chronicles 7:14 (KJV)